Igor's Kitchen

Book #3 In The Ironborn Saga
by Andrew Cavanagh
© 2024 all rights reserved

Chapter 1
Office 451

Crutch and the marines stood at the front entrance of the Office of His Majesty's Royal Navy.

'Says on this piece of paper we need to go to office 451, whatever that is,' said Sergeant Zander.

When they went through the towering double doors of the navy office, the foyer had six armed navy guards in full dress uniform. The marines went up to the long wooden desk at the back of the room. A stern man in spectacles was looking down at papers in front of him.

'Office 451,' said Sergeant Zander.

The head of the man in spectacles shot up. 'Show me.' He held out his hand.

Sergeant Zander stood mute for a few seconds.

'I think he wants the paper,' said Crutch.

'Oh.'

The man in spectacles looked at the paper then looked up at the marines.

'I recognise you now. You are the heroes of the Kona Track.' Most people who said that showed some enthusiasm. He was totally deadpan. Not even a glimmer of emotion. He waved over a guard. 'Corporal Markham, take these men to office 451.' He handed the paper back to Sergeant Zander.

'Yes, sir,' said the corporal. He looked at Crutch and smiled. 'It would be an honour, sir.'

'I know that Sergeant Zander loves honeysap rum and buys grade three to save some coin. But if I want to make my acquaintance with you sergeant, I would buy you a big old mug of premium.'

'By the gods,' said Sergeant Zander.

'Listen to me closely,' said Jasper. 'In espionage, nobody is who they seem to be, and every question, every interaction can be a test or a trap. Make one mistake behind enemy lines, and you'll all be dead. Do you understand?'

'Yes sir.'

'Just call me Jasper. I will tell you one thing and only one thing about myself that is true. I am a master of espionage.'

'You're a spy then?' said Sergeant Zander.

'Espionage goes way beyond being a spy.'

'What's the difference?'

'Subtlety, the clever manipulation of information, and of the people around you. And that difference is what will keep you alive on your mission.'

'You already know our mission?' said Quicksilver.

'I already covered that Quicksilver. Do try to keep up.'

'What do we need to know to stay alive in Estov… on our mission?' said Sergeant Zander.

'You, Sergeant Zander, rely on the predictability of soldiers in battle to get the better of them in unconventional combat. People can be just as predictable in their day-to-day lives if you study them and understand them.'

'How is that going to help us get the… get what we've been sent for?'

'Civil unrest. The people of Estovia are unhappy. The war means food and other essentials are in short supply. It's like a cooking pot over a blast furnace, ready to boil over.'

'And after we make the pot boil over. What do we do after that?'

'I will show you how to stoke the fire. How you achieve the rest of your mission is up to you.'

'I'm a pumpkin,' said Boulder, smiling.

Jasper spent the next two hours teaching the marines about the basics of espionage. Most of it seemed to involve stories of people on missions behind enemy lines making simple errors that led to them being tortured, or killed, or both. Jasper often went into specific, gory detail about how the torture and executions were carried out.

After two hours of imagining himself having hot pokers shoved under his fingernails, thorns inserted into his eyeballs, and four galloping horses ripping his body into multiple parts, Crutch was happy to call it a day.

'We'll continue with this tomorrow,' said Jasper after telling them the day's training was at an end.

'Do we have to?' said Sergeant Zander.

'I'm afraid so,' said Jasper. 'Today I taught you about some of the risks; tomorrow the topic will be different.'

'What's tomorrow's topic?' said Longshot. 'How to survive after your entrails have been cut from your body?'

'Not quite,' said Jasper. 'You'll find out tomorrow. One important rule. Never talk about this training or Office 451 with anyone. Not ever.'

That night when they were alone on the deck of the Auld Faithful, Crutch talked to Cedric. It was Cedric who gave them the written order to go to Office 451, so Crutch figured he must know something about it already.

'Did you know about Office 451?' said Crutch.

'Yes,' said Cedric. 'Every Ironborn commander and most ships' captains know it exists, even though officially it doesn't exist. I assume you were told never to talk about it with anyone?'

'We were. Did you ever meet anyone from the office?'

'I'm not sure. Once I had an Estovian who gave me a piece of paper with Office 451 written on it and a name below that.'

'Do you remember the name?'

'No. It was over twenty years ago.'

'So what did you do?'

'What we were instructed to do at the time. I put him in the brig, kept him under twenty-four hour guard, and handed him and the piece of paper over to the navy office when we reached port in Ironbay.'

'It didn't matter that he was Estovian and you were at war with Estovia?'

'It wouldn't matter if he was the emperor. The instructions were very clear.'

'Do you think Office 451 could have something to do with who's trying to get us killed?'

'You'd know more about that than me. You've been there. What do you think?'

'I really don't know,' said Crutch. 'I'm hoping we'll get some more answers on our little mission tonight.'

'I know you and Sergeant Zander know what you're doing, but be careful,' said Cedric.

Chapter 2
Fancy Purple Shirts

After midnight, Crutch and the marines hid in the alley, looking up at the first-floor window of a sleazy, run down building. A light flared as someone lit a candle inside, and the marines moved, climbing up the ladder on the wall. Crutch went first. Just below him, Longshot threw a grappling hook to the window and secured the rope to the ladder.

Crutch grabbed the rope and climbed hand over hand to the window just as Caleb was coming to see why a grappling hook was on his window sill. He saw Crutch, and fear filled his eyes. He turned and ran for the door.

Crutch was through the window and on top of him before he got there. He held a knife to Caleb's throat as the rest of the marines came through the window.

'Please don't kill me,' said Caleb.

'Tell us what we want to know, and we'll let you live,' said Crutch.

'Try to hold back, and it'll be the last thing you do,' said Sergeant Zander.

'I'll tell you anything,' said Caleb, starting to sob.

'Oh, for pity's sake. Why do the pathetic worms always have to cry?' said Sergeant Zander. 'Spoils the whole mood of a good interrogation. Get him up.'

Boulder helped Crutch get Caleb to his feet. They sat him in an old chair with a split down its wooden seat. The room was tiny and smelled rotten. The marines were crowded into the only empty space between the door and the window. The rest of the room was taken up with a narrow bed with dirty sheets.

'Look at where your life as a lying rat has brought you, Caleb,' said Sergeant Zander. 'Your mother must be proud.'

'My mother's dead.'

'Probably died of shame when she found out what you did.'

'I'm sorry. I didn't know what to do. They said they'd set me free if I told 'em what they wanted.'

'Who said?'

'Which arsehole in the navy office wanted us dead?'

'It weren't a navy guy?'

'What?'

'It weren't a navy guy. The man had all fancy clothes, like he was from the palace.'

'Someone from the palace? Sounds like you're making stuff up, Caleb.' Sergeant Zander motioned to Boulder, who moved in and pulled back his fist, ready to strike.

'I'm not making it up, I swear! The man talked really posh, and he was wearing fancy robes, and he said if I told the magistrate what he said, then they'd give me a nice job in the navy office and a nice place to live, and now look at where I am. They lied to me.'

Sergeant Zander looked at Crutch and raised his eyebrows. 'You better not be lying to us,' said Sergeant Zander.

'I'm not lying!'

'Do you remember his name?'

'Never told me his name.'

'How convenient.'

'He had two guards with him. Palace guards. With those fancy purple shirts.'

'King's guards,' said Crutch. He'd seen them when he was a street urchin. You gave them a wide berth. If a street urchin got anywhere near them, they'd throw you into a wall or elbow you in the face to get you out of their way.

'Someone from the palace with two king's guards then?'

'I'm not believing any of this,' said Longshot.

'I swear it's true,' said Caleb, snot coming out of his nose. 'Why would I lie to you?'

'Same reason you liked to the magistrate,' said Crutch. 'To save your own arse.'

Despite several more attempts at intimidation, Caleb wouldn't budge on his story. The marines left the way they came, taking their grappling hook with them once they got to the ladder. As they slipped out of the dark alley, Crutch thought he saw something move behind him out of the corner of his eye, but when he looked back, there was nothing there.

Later at the Auld Faithful, the marines and Cedric talked about what Caleb had told them.

'I don't know what to make of it,' said Sergeant Zander.

'It doesn't make any sense,' said Crutch. 'Why would someone at the palace want us dead?'

'And if they did,' said Quicksilver, 'why not just send one of their guards or their assassins to take us out quietly in the night.'

'We were in jail the first time around,' said Crutch. 'Hard to kill someone without being noticed in a cell full of prisoners.'

'But now they could take us out any time they wanted to. When we're walking in the streets of Ironbay or taking a piss in the middle of the night.'

'The real answer,' said Cedric, 'may lie behind who they want dead and why.'

'Any ideas?'

'Not yet,' said Cedric. 'But whoever it is, I think the appearance of things is critically important to them.'

'So whoever it is, they don't want word to get out in Ironbay that we were found in a dark alley with our throats cut.'

'So it would seem,' said Cedric.

'But execution as pirates or dying in a heroic last stand on the Kona Track is just fine.'

'Exactly. It appears they don't want any possibility of an investigation or suspicion of wrongdoing coming back on them.'

'So they have something to hide?' said Crutch.

'It would appear so. Something to do with us that makes our very existence a hazardous inconvenience to them.'

'And now we're being sent into the heart of Estovia to bring back the one thing the magnificent Igor Solokov wants to hold on to more than anything else in his empire.'

Chapter 3
Disguise

The next day at Office 451, Jasper greeted them with one word.

'Clumsy.'

'What's that, Jasper?' said Sergeant Zander.

'Clumsy.'

'I'm still not following you.'

'Your little interrogation of Caleb from the navy office. Clumsy, unprofessional, and inept to the point of incompetence.'

'How did you know?' said Quicksilver. Jasper frowned at him. 'Oh.'

'You could have had a third party ply him with drinks and extract any information he had. You could have listened in to his conversations with his friends and colleagues. You could have just knocked on his door and talked to him.

'Instead, you climb through a window in an alley and assault him, ensuring that anyone who sees you brands every one of you as a criminal or a spy. And now he's so terrified, you'll never get him to speak openly to you. Clumsy. The kind of schoolboy caper that gets you killed in the field.'

'I'm a pumpkin,' said Boulder.

'At least one of you understands his level of competence,' said Jasper.

After their dressing down, Jasper moved on to his lesson for the day.

'Disguise. The secret to disguise is blending in. Being exactly what people in an area are used to seeing. Most of the people you'll be interacting with are poor.' Jasper looked at their tattered marine uniforms, still torn and stained from the Kona Track. 'I see you've got the peasant look down.'

'I don't think these marine uniforms will cut it,' said Sergeant Zander. 'No matter how ragged they are.'

'You're right. But blending in isn't just about the clothes you wear. It's also about the way you speak and act. We need to give you personas that blend in. Everything has to match.'

'We could be travelling minstrels,' said Longshot. 'I can sing.'

'I can do a bit of a fire show behind him to add some spice,' said Quicksilver.

'The objective is to keep eyes off you,' said Jasper, 'not to draw attention to yourselves by lighting up your path with flames.'

Quicksilver looked disappointed.

'Well, Longshot can still sing.'

'Give me a song then,' said Jasper.

Longshot sang three words, and Jasper said, 'And now you're being dragged off by the Teevilgrad Watch for your execution.'

'I was enjoying that.'

'His singing wasn't that bad,' said Quicksilver.

'Yes, at least one of those notes was in key, but that big old Ironbay accent is somewhat of an impediment if you want to stay alive in Teevilgrad. Can any of you speak with an Estovian accent?'

'That'd be Crutch,' said Sergeant Zander.

'Crutch's Estovian is so good, the Estovians are jealous of his accent.'

'Let me hear it,' said Jasper.

'Is not accent Ironworm. Is you who can't talk proper.'

Jasper smiled. 'Well, one of you has some talent. Can anyone else do an Estovian accent?'

'I did it once in Zanithburg,' said Sergeant Zander.

'How well did that work?'

'Three hundred Estovians tried to kill us,' said Quicksilver

'Three hundred?'

'Okay, it might have been more like six hundred,' said Sergeant Zander.

'Now I have to hear it.'

'Really?'

'Goodness yes.'

Sergeant Zander put on his best talking pose. 'Hello compatriot. Fine day today, what?'

It was so awful, Crutch and Jasper cringed with every butchered word.

'Dreadful,' said Jasper. 'I feel like killing you myself. Anyone else?'

Quicksilver and Longshot shook their heads.

Jasper looked at Boulder hopefully.

'I'm a pumpkin.'

Jasper raised his eyebrows. 'It appears Crutch will be doing the talking then.'

'There might be a problem with that,' said Sergeant Zander.

'Go on.'

'The Estovians have seen Crutch when he helped break the siege of Ironbay and when he led the troops on the Kona Track. Seeing a crippled boy with a cane might set off some alarms.'

'Good point,' said Jasper, stroking his moustache and thinking. 'Crutch, can you pretend to be an old Estovian man for me?'

Crutch thought about it. He pictured old man Jim from his time as a street urchin.

'Thank you, compatriot.' He coughed like he was hacking up half a lung. 'My old bones don't walk like young man.' He hobbled forward, his back hunched over. 'Eyes are dim too.' He moved his cane from side to side as if he was checking the ground in front of him before walking forward.

'Might be overdoing it a little there, Crutch, but I can see this working. Just need to find a way to hide your talentless companions in plain sight. That's quite the obstacle.'

'I don't know about that,' said Quicksilver. 'A few more lessons from you, and we'll be espoynabarging with the best of 'em.'

'I'm a pumpkin,' said Boulder.

Jasper wrote some instructions on how to disguise the Auld Faithful, that Sergeant Zander passed on to Cedric. While they were training, the ship was repainted. Workers painted over its name. New sails were made and stored below deck.

The added a new, gaudy-looking figurehead of a naked lady to the bow. Some of the more rowdy crewmen liked it, but Cedric hated it. One thing was certain: it made the Auld Faithful look very different.

Many changes, like the change of sails, were to be implemented once they were at sea to avoid spies in Ironbay taking notice of a ship in port suddenly turning into something you'd expect in an Estovian port.

Jasper suggested calling her the Flying Lady in any interactions with Estovians, but they didn't paint on the name for the same reason. They didn't want Estovian spies to report that to someone in Teevilgrad. In Crutch's mind, she'd always be the Auld Faithful, no matter what they renamed her to.

Most of the changes reverted the ship back to looking like a merchant vessel, including the removal of the two ballistas on the front deck. This made Crutch and the marines nervous.

'We're at the mercy of any ship with heavy armaments now,' said Sergeant Zander.

'And we'll be in Estovian territory with no way to defend ourselves,' said Longshot.

'Jasper says once we're in Estovian waters, our only real defence is avoiding discovery,' said Crutch.

'What's worries me the most,' said Sergeant Zander, 'is that he's right. Apart from you, Crutch, we've never been that great at pulling off a deception. Our real talents lie in running and fighting our way out when things go pear-shaped.'

'Or setting everything on fire, then running for it,' said Quicksilver.

'Once we're in Estovia, if we say one word at the wrong time, we could all die,' said Longshot.

'Or end up back in prison.'

Thoughts of their time living on cockroaches in the Zanithburg prison still brought real pain. They all carried the scars of Zanithburg with them, Quicksilver most of all. He'd grown his hair long to cover his missing ear. When the wind blew, you could see the cuts where his ear used to be. Crutch hoped their disguises wouldn't be blown away as easily once they were in Zanithburg.

Chapter 4
The Arms Of An Angel

Crutch pulled on the oars of the longboat in the Ironbay harbour as Abagail sat smiling at him in the stern holding the tiller, wearing a thin white summer dress that rippled in the sea breeze. There was a lantern at the bow of the boat, so they could see in the darkness.

'You have to move that tiller the opposite way to the one you want the boat to go in,' said Crutch.

'I'm an admiral's daughter,' said Abagail. 'I've sailed a boat before.'

'Sorry,' said Crutch. 'Of course you have. It's just that there's a warship coming up right behind us.'

Abagail looked around, saw the ship lit up with lanterns, and pulled the tiller hard towards her. The ship cleared them safely, ringing its bell.

One of the crew yelled, 'Is that you, Corporal Crutch?'

'It is,' yelled back Crutch.

'Fought with you in the siege of Ironbay. Greatest honour of my life.'

'The honour was mine,' yelled Crutch.

'You have a wonderful night. Your girl looks gorgeous.'

'Thank you,' yelled Crutch.

'Thank you,' said Abagail, beaming.

'You do look gorgeous,' said Crutch as he pulled on the oars. 'Like an angel with the deepest blue eyes and the prettiest smile in the world.

Abagail laughed. 'That was like poetry.'

'I just made it up then when I was looking at you.'

'Can you make up more like that?'

'Why?' said Crutch.

'I could listen to it all night long.'

They were away from the lights of the docks so Crutch stopped rowing and let the boat drift. The harbour was nearly perfectly calm tonight.

'Mother would like you to come to dinner,' said Abagail.

'Will the admiral be there?' said Crutch.

'Of course. Mother has never really met you properly, and she'd like to talk to you and see what you're like.'

Crutch looked reluctant. He was fairly certain it would also mean he'd be eating with fancy plates and spoons and rules for acting the nobles had, that he knew nothing about.

'There'll be food and pastries for dessert,' said Abagail.

'I'll be there,' said Crutch without even thinking.

Abagail laughed. 'On that note, I brought cake and pastries,' said Abagail. There was a picnic hamper on the seat next to her.

'Why don't you come sit with me here and we can eat them together,' said Crutch.

'Okay.'

Crutch helped her move the picnic hamper, their bodies moving against each other as Crutch got the hamper, put it on the bottom of the boat and Abagail sat next to him, the touch of her body sending tingles through him.

Abagail opened the hamper.

'Cake?' she said, handing Crutch a piece.

Crutch bit the huge piece she gave him once, then swallowed it.

Abagail laughed. 'I don't know how you do that. It's not natural.'

Crutch grinned.

Abagail opened the other side of the hamper. 'Pastries?' She handed him a pastry, and he didn't even bite it; just swallowed it in one gulp. Abagail laughed.

There was a flapping of wings, and Crutch pointed, 'Look. A flock of seagulls.'

When Abagail turned her head, Crutch jammed as many pastries as he could get into his pockets. When she turned back, he was looking at her, smiling in a way that was so innocent it made him look guilty.

She looked down at the hamper, now almost empty of pastries, looked at his pockets, and laughed.

'You are hilarious,' she said as she leaned into him, putting her hand on his chest.

Crutch smiled. 'And you are wonderful.'

They sat that way for a beautiful moment, staring up at the clear night sky, just enjoying being with each other, their bodies close, the cool, gentle sea breeze on their skin.

'Did your father ever teach you about the stars?' said Crutch.

'No, he didn't.'

'The stars in the sky are like magic. If you can read them, you know exactly where you are in the world.'

'Really?' said Abagail.

'Yes. See that really big set of stars there? That's the Ironborn Cross. It always points south.'

'It's so bright.'

'That's why we use it for navigation.'

'See that curve of stars there, like a bow a hunter uses.'

'The curve? Wait. Yes, I see it.'

'That's the hunter's bow. Then you take that big star there and the big star at the other end and draw a line; it's like a bow and arrow. They call that the Archer constellation. It points west.'

'That's amazing.'

'And see that group of bright stars all bunched up together in a figure of eight.' Crutch ran his finger in front of him across the group of stars.

'Yes, I see it. Where does that point?'

'It doesn't point anywhere. They call that the Lover's Knot because you can happily follow it around for eternity and not care, like two lovers adrift in the sea.'

'That's beautiful,' said Abagail, sliding her arm around his waist. 'And looking up at those stars, can you tell me where you are now?'

'Yes. In the arms of an angel.'

Chapter 5
Dressing A Pumpkin

At Office 451 Jasper had sent off the marines for an hour so he could work with Crutch alone.

'This is face paint,' said Jasper. 'You use it to disguise your appearance. You'll be posing as an old man, so you need your skin to look aged.' Jasper opened the large jar he had and started smearing the pale yellow-brown paste onto Crutch's face.

'It smells like bad breath and piss,' said Crutch.

'Yes. Wonderful, isn't it? The scent is my own addition. When you wear it, it not only makes you look like an old man, it makes you smell like one too.'

'Do you ever use this face paint?' said Crutch.

'The nobles have a saying, 'A woman never reveals her secrets.''

Crutch laughed.

'To pass as an old man, it's not enough to look and act like an old man. You need to think like an old man too.'

'In what way?'

'As you get old, your body changes. You have to piss more often. Sometimes you feel like you desperately need to take a piss, but nothing comes out. You're terrified of simple things like walking down a long flight of stairs.'

Crutch nodded. He immediately saw how getting into the mind of an older person could help him pull off the disguise.

'Probably most important of all, the things you care about change. Young people have dreams of the future. Dreams for themselves. Most people never stop dreaming, but old people have dreams for other people. They live their dreams through their family or close friends.'

'So I need to be the kind, helpful old man?'

'Exactly.'

'Sounds like fun.'

'It can be, but it's very easy to drop your guard and make a mistake. Then you all die. 'Old men have one other advantage.'

'What's that?' said Crutch.

'They can blend into the background. No one wants to look at an old man hobbling around with a cane, taking an age to get from his home to the store. They don't want to remind themselves they'll be limping around like that someday.'

'I'm familiar with that. No one wants to look at a street urchin.'

'Yes, it's similar. But there are also kind people who will help you. They can be a real threat to you if you're not careful.'

'Why?'

'If your disguise isn't perfect, including everything you say and do, they might see through it.'

'Right.'

'There's one more thing old men do that young men don't,' said Jasper. They think constantly about their deaths. They know death is coming. They can feel it in their bodies. They just don't know when.'

'I lived with that as a street urchin too.'

'Yes, but it's different when you're old. There is no hope you'll survive somehow. Time is something you no longer have to look forward to. It's your greatest enemy.' Jasper finished applying the face paint to his nose, then picked up a mirror so Crutch could see.

'By the gods!' He looked like an old man. His face was splotchy, from pale yellow spots to darker, aged skin. He was wonderfully, horribly old. It was like looking in the mirror and seeing himself seventy years from now.

'This face paint will last weeks on your skin, but you should reapply it over any missing spots every day. Put it on all your exposed skin. You don't want your face to look ninety and your hands to look like a teenagers.

'The paint is tough, but if you get saltwater on it then rub it hard, it will go a little more runny so you can get it off.'

'So I shouldn't go swimming in the ocean then dry off with a towel?' said Crutch.

'Not unless you want to get it off in a hurry.'

When the other marines returned, they looked at Crutch like their eyes were playing tricks on them.

'By the gods,' said Sergeant Zander. 'What happened to you while we were out?'

'Must be some kind of magic,' said Quicksilver.

'Not magic, just face paint,' said Crutch.

'You need to eat more greens,' said Boulder.

'Greens?'

'Grandma says, if you don't eat your greens, your skin will get old and wrinkled.'

'Based on that, you look like you sat in the sun for a hundred years and never had a single blade of spinach,' said Longshot.

'Now we need to work on your clothes,' said Jasper. 'All your clothes. That shouldn't be too hard. Just need to change your stained, torn Ironborn peasant clothes, to stained, torn, drab Estovian peasant clothes.'

'Peasant clothes?' said Sergeant Zander. 'These are our navy uniforms.'

'Yes. I'd say they've seen better days, but that would be an insult to the common language. I've seen piles of garbage that have better clothes in them than what you're wearing.'

'So now we have to start digging through garbage piles?' said Quicksilver.

'That would be an improvement,' said Jasper, 'but I think we can do a little better than that.'

'I'm a pumpkin,' said Boulder.

'You need work to pull that off. A pumpkin is better dressed,' said Jasper.

Chapter 6
Orange Rock

At the morning meal in the galley, Cedric sat with the marines.

'We leave after final loading tomorrow,' he said.

'So no slipping out before dawn, so we're not seen?' said Sergeant Zander.

'No. The navy office wants us to leave like any other ship in the full light of day. Trying to slip away quietly might arouse suspicion with spies keeping an eye on the docks.'

Jasper wasn't happy this would be their last day of training. Jasper and Crutch knew they weren't ready to go into the heart of Estovia and pass as locals, but they'd just have to do the best they could and find a way to survive.

'Today we talk about assets,' said Jasper.

'You mean gold, gems, and the like?' said Sergeant Zander.

'No. Assets in espionage are the people you can use to further your ends.'

'So your allies?'

'That is one type of asset. A person who knows who you really are. They're often the most dangerous type of asset. If they get caught, you're exposed. You escape immediately, or your imprisonment or execution is inevitable.'

'What are the other types of assets?' said Crutch.

'The most valuable assets are contacts you build who don't know who you really are. Ideally, you can manipulate them, and they never find out.'

'How do you do that?'

'Appeal to their baser motivations. Greed, patriotism, love, family.'

'So you work out what's important to them, and then you use that to get them to do what you want?' said Crutch.

'Exactly. These can be every-day people with ordinary lives. Every city is full of people who go unseen and have access to important people or resources. Servants, assistants, secret lovers, whores, gong farmers.'

'Gong farmers?' said Quicksilver.

'They collect rich people's shit out of their privies,' said Crutch.

'How do you know so much about shit?' said Quicksilver.

'I grew up in the sewers,' said Crutch.

'You use these people to mine information,' said Jaspser. 'Or to plant information where people can find it, to get you incriminating evidence, to start fires, to start fights, to spread lies.'

'I prefer to start my own fires,' said Quicksilver.

'What do you do if they figure out who you are?' said Longshot.

'Dispose of the body where it won't be found.'

'You kill them?'

'I thought that went without saying. You could also frame someone for their murder or try to make it look like they died of natural causes, but that's unreliable. If dead bodies start appearing around you, it brings suspicion you really don't need.'

'What if they're innocent, every-day people?' said Crutch.

'Most will be innocent. If you let them live, you can usually measure your own life in hours.'

That was a sobering thought. Crutch did not want to have to kill more innocents.

'There is another type of asset. Someone sent to you from the home office who knows who you are. They'll use your password to identify themselves. Your password is orange rock.'

'Like glowstone,' said Sergeant Zander.

'Exactly.'

Jasper spent the next few hours going into details and telling stories about how assets could be manipulated, how you could use them, and the mistakes you could make doing it. He ended telling several new stories in graphic detail about how people using espionage techniques had come to a grisly end.

'Don't trust anyone; always keep your guard up; don't share any information you don't need to; and brains before brawn. Crutch, you're one of the most talented students of espionage I've ever seen.' Jasper looked at Sergeant Zander. 'Any time you're unsure, you should trust Crutch's judgement.'

'We already do,' said Sergeant Zander.

'Very wise. This is our last training session, so I hope to see you alive again someday.'

'If we make it back to Ironbay alive, I'll shout you an ale,' said Sergeant Zander.

'If you're alive the next time I see you, I'll buy you a mug of honeysap premium,' said Jasper.

'I'd like that,' said Sergeant Zander, smiling. He shook Jasper's hand. 'Thank you for your help.'

Before they left, Jasper took Crutch aside. 'I need to show you something.' Jasper rubbed at the palm of his right hand and revealed a tattoo there. 'Take a close look.'

Crutch leaned in and saw it was a faded heart in intricate detail with the name Rosee written below it.

'If you ever need to identify me in the field, you can check for this tattoo.'

Crutch didn't understand. 'Identify you?'

'It's likely I'll be wearing a disguise.'

Crutch nodded.

'You're going into an enemy city in the middle of a war. You'll need to use everything you've got to get you and your marines out of this alive, Crutch. Most of the success of this mission will depend on you.'

Crutch was anxious as it was. Jasper had just taken him over the edge into fear.

'If anyone can pull this off, it will be you,' said Jasper. 'Good luck.'

'Thank you,' said Crutch, shaking Jasper's hand.

Chapter 7
Conversating

The marines gathered at a table in the galley.

'I could use your advice,' said Crutch.

'Whatever you need,' said Sergeant Zander.

'We're always here for you, Crutch.'

'Abagail has invited me to dinner with her parents.'

'The admiral?'

'Yes, and her mother, Lady Hastings.'

'A dinner with a lord and a lady. No pressure.'

'Don't tell 'em you grew up in the sewers. That's a good way to start,' said Longshot.

'You know,' said Quicksilver, 'you might not want to mention the sewers at all. It's up to you, but that might not be good dinner conversation for a lord and a lady.'

'Maybe wear your dress uniform,' said Sergeant Zander. 'Is it still in good nick?'

'It is.' For the first time ever, Crutch had a uniform for more than twenty-four hours that wasn't covered in muck, or blood, or both.

'Well, that will help.'

'You know how you stuff pastries, and bread, and other food in your pockets?' said Longshot.

'Yes.'

'Could you get enough pastries for all of us this time? Last time, there weren't enough to go around.'

All the marines nodded and agreed with that.

'I like pastries,' said Boulder.

'Any tips on eating?' said Crutch.

'They lay out all these fancy silver forks, and knives, and spoons,' said Sergeant Zander.

'Right.'

'They put these little ones on the outside and big ones on the inside. They're all really shiny.'

'Right.'

'So my advice to you is to just look at all that silver cutlery but don't take any of it,' said Sergeant Zander. 'Doesn't matter how much you'd like to have a souvenir of your fancy meal. Those nobles get really upset when you take their silver spoons.'

'You've got that right,' said Longshot. 'Remember that do at Lord Seerbrucker's mansion. It was all, 'You've stolen my best spoons you thieves.' Then they were throwing us out before we even had a chance to finish our desserts.'

'So definitely don't take any of their fancy silver spoons, no matter how good they look.'

'And if you do, don't get caught.'

'Any advice on conversation?'

'Yeh, you probably shouldn't do that.'

'I shouldn't do what.'

'Conversate,' said Quicksilver. 'It can only lead to trouble. I was at this lord's place, and they got me conversating. I was explaining how I set a group of enemy guards on fire and how the smell when they burnt was so strong and all the women started retching. I'm fairly certain there was something wrong with the fish, but my girlfriend told me it was because of my bad conversating. So yeah, give that a miss.'

'Just sit there, keep your hands off the fancy silver, and don't say nothing. That's the safest bet.'

Later Crutch talked to Boulder.

'You're better than the other marines at this kind of advice,' said Crutch. 'Do you have any tips for me?'

Boulder grinned. 'I'm a pumpkin.'

Chapter 8
A Pocket Full Of Pastries

Crutch sat at the dinner table with Abagail on his left, Admiral Hastings at the head of the table, and Abagail's mother, Lady Hastings at the other end. Servants brought out the first course of the meal, some kind of tiny bird by the look of it.

Crutch watched Abagail pick up the tiny fork and knife from the outside of a small collection of cutlery around her plate. He looked at his plate and did the same. She saw he was looking at her and smiled.

There wasn't much bird. It was only as big as a tiny rat, but it tasted delicious. No bits of feathers to mash up with his teeth, and nothing got stuck in his teeth when he swallowed. Crutch looked up and realised they were all watching him, including the two servants, one woman and one man, standing at attention next to the table.

Abagail's eyes had a glint in them, and she tried unsuccessfully to conceal a conspiratorial grin.

The next course was fish with yam and beans and had some kind of fancy greens over the top of the fish. They tasted a bit funny, all mixed together in his mouth, but they were still good. Crutch managed to wolf the whole meal down in three large mouthfuls. He looked up when he finished to see everyone at the table looking at him again.

'Hungry then?' said Admiral Hastings.

'Young men can have quite the appetite,' said Lady Hastings. 'You can't hold that against Crutch.'

'I'm quite familiar with young men's appetites,' said the admiral. 'I was somewhat hoping Corporal Crutch would see fit to curb his when he was in the presence of my daughter.'

Abagail grinned, then broke into a laugh.

'What's so funny, dear,' said Lady Hastings.

'Crutch eats like that to entertain me. You should have seen how he and the marines drank and ate on the Auld Faithful. Forking in slabs of pork and sculling full mugs of rum. Crutch's friend Boulder made the most hilarious show of letting out a huge belch.'

Lady Hastings put her hand on her chest and looked at Abagail with shock on her face.

'How do you know how the marines on the Auld Faithful eat?' said the admiral.

'Crutch was kind enough to invite me on board for a morning meal,' said Abagail.

There was a long silence as the admiral stared at Abagail. She dropped her head and looked down at her plate as the silence became more uncomfortable.

'Corporal Crutch. Why did you think it would be a good idea to take my daughter onto a navy ship?'

'I was just trying to be hospitable, admiral.'

'So you took my fourteen-year-old daughter into the galley of a navy ship where the crew were drinking rum?'

Crutch had to admit it sounded bad when he put it like that.

'It wasn't all that bad. Everyone was friendly, and Abagail only had one mug.'

'You gave her rum?'

'Please don't raise your voice at the dinner table, dear,' said Lady Hastings.

'Raise my voice? Raise my voice? Corporal Crutch thought it would be acceptable to take my daughter on a ship full of drunk sailors and ply her with rum. He'll be lucky if I don't have him flogged!'

'It wasn't like that,' said Abagail. 'They were very polite. Captain Beaumont was there.'

'Captain Beaumont? Cedric, the king of bloody pirates, Beaumont?'

'Cedric was never a pirate,' said Crutch.

'There are reliable witnesses who say otherwise.'

'Caleb Johnson is a stinking liar,' said Crutch.

'You can't deny you were pirates,' said the admiral.

'William Wyld forced us into piracy. Cedric risked his life to beat Wyld in a duel to take back the Auld Faithful.'

'This pantomime has gone far enough,' said the admiral. 'What kind of life do you think Corporal Crutch can give you?'

'I don't care,' said Abagail.

'You'll care when you're trying to raise his child in a filthy two-room hovel stinking of the sewers.'

'If I'm with Crutch, I won't.'

'Wake up, girl. You can't build a life with a crippled commoner from the streets.'

The anger built in Crutch. He couldn't stand to see anyone attacking Abagail. He had to fight back.

'You didn't mind me being a cripple or a commoner when I saved you from the Estovians at Abagail's birthday party. Or when you sent me to die on the Kona Track.'

'And somehow you weren't smart enough to oblige me,' said the admiral.

For several seconds, they sat in stunned silence.

'You sent Crutch to die?' said Abagail.

The admiral looked at the pain on Abagail's face. It stopped him, like someone had punched him in the guts. Something Crutch would love to do right now.

'It wasn't like that,' said the admiral.

'Crutch was the only boy who was ever kind to me,' said Abagail, a single tear running down her cheek. 'He's the only boy who ever said I was pretty and meant it.'

Across from them, the young lady servant started sobbing and ran out of the room.

'Now look what you've done,' said Lady Hastings. 'Could you please finish this meal without any more attacks on our guest or your daughter?'

Admiral Hastings held up his knife with his mouth open, ready to say something, thought better of it and nodded his assent.

'My apologies, Crutch,' said Lady Hastings, throwing a stern look at the admiral. 'I hope we can all show you a little more common courtesy than you've seen so far tonight.'

The admiral glared at Crutch, and Crutch glared right back.

Crutch felt like he should storm out of the room and the house, like they did in some of the novels Cedric had him read. But he didn't want to upset Abagail any more than she was already. And dessert was still coming. He found Abagail's hand under the table and squeezed it, and she squeezed back while she wiped the tear from her face.

After dessert came, when no one was looking, Crutch stuffed his pockets full of as many pastries as he could get into them.

Chapter 9

Goodbye

The next day, the Auld Faithful made its final preparations before leaving. The ship was unrecognisable with its new paint work and its ballistas removed. They had even changed some of the fittings.

Families of the crew were on the docks, saying goodbye for the last hour. Crutch kept looking for Abagail, but she wasn't there. The last twenty minutes, he stood at the rail and waited for her to come, but she didn't come.

When Cedric called for the crew to free the mooring lines, Crutch almost hoped that she'd come running down the docks at the last moment, breathless and apologetic. But there was no last-minute appearance, no last-minute apology.

Cedric ordered the crew to make sail, and Crutch still stood at the rail watching the docks. She simply wasn't there. He had to accept the fact that she didn't come, that she would never come again. He'd lost her. That was the only possible conclusion. As the Auld Faithful pulled away from the docks, it was like his heart was still there, waiting on the docks, hoping for Abagail and being ripped from his body.

Boulder came to his side and put his hand on Crutch's shoulder.

'Abagail?' said Boulder.

Crutch nodded. 'She didn't come. To say goodbye.'

'You can still hope,' said Boulder.

'I think it's too late for hope.'

'It hurts your heart?' said Boulder.

'Yes.'

There was a long moment of silence, then he said, 'One day it won't hurt any more.'

'Thank you, Boulder.'

'You're my friend,' said Boulder.

Chapter 10
Running Silent

Once they were inside enemy waters, Cedric gave the order that talking should be kept to an absolute minimum. A passing Estovian ship, or fisherman, or someone on shore who heard Ironborn accents might raise the alarm, then they'd have Estovian warships swarming all over them.

Cedric ordered the crew to talk as quietly as possible while on deck and the lookouts to use their whistles to communicate sightings. Below deck, the crew could talk, but softly enough that they couldn't be heard up top.

The silence on the deck gave the Auld Faithful an eerie feel. It felt like one of the ghost ships Crutch had read about, moving silently through the waves with ghosts at the helm and on the rigging.

Their first night in enemy territory Crutch was with the marines in the galley when he heard scraping on the hull. They climbed the ladders onto the deck where deck hands were holding lanterns to look over the side.

'Wooden stakes under the water,' whispered one deck hand to Cedric. Cedric joined the marines on the rail to see for himself.

'Sea defences,' whispered Cedric. 'The Estovian ships have these marked on their charts, so they know where they are. Without charts, we'll have to find our own way through. Silently.'

'We can go down the side of the hull on ropes and use hand signals to let you know which way to go,' whispered Sergeant Zander.

'Do it. I've sailed through these kinds of defences before. I can only slow the ship down so much. Too slow, and the waves and currents will push her onto the stakes.'

Crutch and Sergeant Zander nodded. So the Auld Faithful would be moving, and they'd have very little time to signal a change in direction.

Crutch went down the starboard bow outside the ship with Boulder on the deck, holding a rope tied to his waist. Sergeant Zander went down the port bow. Deckhands held lanterns over the rails so they could see.

Almost as soon as they lowered him over the rail, out of the dark, Crutch could see wooden stakes coming high out of the water. The top stakes were over the level of his head. He signalled furiously to the deckhand with the lantern to get the ship to change tacks.

The stakes came at him fast. He was almost on them when the ship changed tack, heeling the other way, and Boulder hauled him up at the same time. Was it enough? The top stake was so close it ripped his pants as it went past, and missed the hull further down by inches.

It's weird what you think about when you're in mortal danger. While searching ahead, Crutch looked at the new figurehead put on the bow in Ironbay and thought, *that is one ugly naked lady*.

Cedric steered the Auld Faithful perfectly between two long lines of thick wooden stakes in the water now. But when he pulled his eyes off the figurehead of the naked lady, up ahead Crutch saw a much bigger problem. A thick net ran from one side of the stakes to the other, blocking their path. If the Auld Faithful ran into it and got trapped, the waves would push the ship onto one line of stakes or the other, ripping the hull to pieces.

Crutch didn't know what to signal. They couldn't stop. The waves would push the ship into the stakes. There wasn't enough room to turn back. They were just a few yards from the stakes on either side of the ship.

Sergeant Zander had told him paralysis would get you killed. *Do something Crutch. Do something.* As they got closer, he saw the net anchored into a rock on each side. Iron bars came out of the rock, and the rope was attached to the iron bars by a chain and shackle. His best chance was to get onto the rock and get that net unshackled.

The wooden stakes got closer to the ship as the Estovian ocean trap funnelled the Auld Faithful to its destruction. If he jumped too soon, a stake would impale him. Jump too short, and he'd hit the side of the rock, fall in the water, and the Auld Faithful would run over him. Jump too late, and the stakes on the other side of the net would stab him.

The most likely outcome from jumping was death. So he jumped.

Not far enough. Crutch landed on the top edge of the rock, but only his arms were on the rock. The rest of his body slid down the side of the rock. As his arms lost their grip and he started to slip over the edge, he looked to his left and saw the rope for the net. He grabbed it with his left hand, dangled at the edge for a second until he grabbed the rope with his other hand, and pulled himself up.

As soon as he was on the rock, he saw another problem. There were two ropes: one rope for the top of the net and one rope for the bottom. He had to disconnect both. He tried the shackle on the top rope as the Auld Faithful hit the net, and it started to bend forward. He couldn't move the shackle with his hands.

He pulled his walking stick out of his belt and hacked at the rope. The tension on the rope got higher as the net moved further forward with the Auld Faithful. He hacked and cut at the top rope, and finally it snapped, whipping by his head and missing his face by inches.

The Auld Faithful was still moving, and there was another problem. He didn't have enough time to cut through the bottom rope with the blade of his walking cane. By the time he got through it, the ship would be caught on the net.

Out of the dim light from the lanterns of the ship, something flew towards him. It landed on the rock at his feet. A huge shackle key! Someone was watching. He picked up the shackle key and took to the pin of the shackle. It was tight and rusted from being in the salt water and salty ocean breeze. Crutch strained at it with everything he had as he could hear the Auld Faithful's hull groaning against the force of the net.

Then the shackle moved. Crutch spun the pin of the shackle round as fast as he could. The instant he got it free, the u-shaped end of the shackle flung out, ripping the rope into the ocean. The Auld Faithful immediately picked up speed as the net washed under it.

The stern of the Auld Faithful was already passing him. He could see Boulder on the deck waving his hands to the rest of the crew. The crew pointed in the water behind the stern of the ship. Then Crutch saw it. A buoy in the water on a line trailing in the water behind the ship. It was about to get to him. He could see Sergeant Zander on the rock on the other side of the ship, ready to jump for a buoy trailing on the other side.

Crutch jammed his walking cane in his belt and used his arms and his good leg to jump. He hit the water hard on his stomach. The force knocked the wind out of him, and he could feel a stinging pain in his skin there.

He felt a surge of fear. Miss that buoy, and he'd be alone in the ocean. At night, they might never find him, and if they did, they might not be able to get to him with the danger of being wrecked on the ocean defences. He saw the buoy coming up fast, just two yards away.

He swam hard, his arms, legs, and lungs burning with the effort. He just made the line and grabbed it with his hands. The force of it yanked his arms and his shoulders hard, and the rope cut into his palms. The force of the water dragged him back until the buoy was under him.

Crutch clung on, arms straining with the effort as waves slapped into him. The crew on the Auld Faithful hauled him in. They had the climbing ropes down by the time he got to the side of the hull, and he crawled up, his arms trembling with fatigue.

By the time he got to the deck, Sergeant Zander was already there, his face filled with relief. He smiled and whispered, 'Nice night for a swim.'

Crutch looked over at Cedric, who put his hand on his heart and puffed out his cheeks as if the weight of the world had lifted from his shoulders.

Chapter 11
Contraband

Cedric gave Crutch two books from his cabin to read. The first was Keeping Spirits Up At Home. Written by an Ironbay writer, the innocuous title of the book disguised the true nature of its content. This book was all about manipulating public opinion with a strategy of often misleading slogans and posters. The strategy helped drum up support in the Ironborn to keep fighting a war, no matter how long or bloody.

The second book, Magnificent Control, Magnificent Victory, was Estovian and truly unsettling. It outlined how to create complete fiction to get Estovians riled up against a common enemy. It talked about targeting small minority groups in the population and labelling them with the blame for problems they had nothing to do with to divert the blame from the ruling empire and its policies.

It talked about communicating total nonsense to the people in slogans repeated so often they'd be convinced they were true. This was a special kind of evil Crutch never knew could even exist. And now he was going to be a part of it, perpetuating and creating his own brand of lies to manipulate the Estovians in Teevilgrad.

After they'd been sailing two days in Estovian water, the lookout blew his whistle four times. A chill went through Crutch. Estovian ship. He retreated below to check his disguise. Crutch saw Boulder.

'Estovian ship,' said Crutch. 'No talking,'
'I'm a pumpkin,' said Boulder.

Crutch was back on deck at the rail as the Estovian ship approached.

'Border patrol,' yelled an Estovian officer. 'Contraband inspection.'

'Welcome compatriots. We have no contraband.' Crutch coughed a little as he stood hunched over on the deck, propped on his walking cane.

'I am Inspector Petrov. Are you captain?'

'I am too old now to captain vessel myself. I am owner, Sergey Crujge. People call me Crujge.' Jasper told them to use names that were close to their own so they'd respond when someone called them, and if someone slipped up and used their real name, it would likely pass without notice. He pronounced his name Crujge, like sludge.

'We come aboard,' said Inspector Petrov as his crew threw grappling hooks and pulled the two ships together. 'You have contraband?'

'Have been out of Estovia six months. Any new contraband since then?'

'Does crocodile shit in water?' said Inspector Petrov as he jumped aboard, and four armed soldiers came with him.

'If I make mistake, I pay fine. But I don't think I have contraband.'

'We see,' said the inspector.

Crutch wondered how long it would take the inspector, or his soldiers, or the gunners pointing half a dozen ballistas from the border patrol ship to realise that the crew were totally silent.

'What you carry in hold?'

'Food, pigs, one crate weapons.'

'Weapons?'

'Swords, spears. Tell me is not contraband now?'

'Not contraband, but tariff now. Show me hold.'

'Of course.' Crutch made a show of climbing and limping down the ladder into the main cargo hold. 'Every year I get older, ladder gets longer.'

If Inspector Petrov got the joke, he didn't react to it. Not a sound. His face was deadpan.

Crutch took Petrov into the hold, pointed out the different cargo there, and showed the inspector the crate of weapons. One of the soldiers opened it, and the inspector looked at the swords on top, lifted one up, and ran his finger along the blade.

'Is nice weapon. Would kill young man easily.' He pointed the blade at Crutch's throat. 'Kill old man even easier.'

Crutch froze. Had Petrov already worked out something was off with the crew of the Auld Faithful? At the edge of his vision, he could see Sergeant Zander and Boulder moving slowly towards them.

'Ocean is dangerous place,' said Petrov. 'People die from disease, fall overboard. Need protection from high place to stay safe.'

'Protection?'

'You old merchant. You understand protection.'

'Oh protection. What is fair price?' said Crutch.

'I feel generous. Fifty rublets.'

'Is fair price, if tariff is small.'

Petrov laughed. 'You smart old merchant. I will reduce tariff to half. But seventy-five rublets for protection.'

'Sixty.'

'I like you, old man. Deal.'

'How much for tariff?'

'Should be one hundred fifty rublets. I make seventy-five.'

'Is good deal,' said Crutch. 'You give tariff papers?'

'Of course.'

'I get you rublets.' Crutch looked at Sergeant Zander. 'Son! Come here!'

Sergeant Zander didn't move.

Crutch pointed straight at Sergeant Zander. 'Idiot son! Come here!'

Sergeant Zander handed Boulder's chain to Longshot and ran up to Crutch. Crutch smacked him on the shins with his walking cane. Sergeant Zander jumped in pain to the laughs of the soldiers and Petrov.

'Next time I call you, come fast. Get me one hundred thirty-five rublets from chest. Get captain to help count. Be quick!'

Sergeant Zander ran off.

'Good help hard to find with war on,' said Crutch. 'How is it for you?'

'Is okay. His magnificence Emperor Solokov loves his tariffs. Plenty men for crew.'

Sergeant Zander returned with the money.

'Do I need to count for you?' said Crutch, taking the small sack of money from Sergeant Zander and handing it to Inspector Petrov.

'No. If amount is wrong, will be much worse for you than me.'

'If amount is wrong, is because idiot son can't count,' said Crutch, slapping Sergeant Zander around the ear. 'Let me know, and I will fix.'

Petrov nodded and smiled. 'Pleasure doing business with you Crujge. If you ever need help, I am Teevilburg border patrol.'

'Help at price?' said Crutch.

'Of course. Have to pay bills and officials. Everyone must be paid.'

After the Estovian ship was gone and the marines were below deck, Crutch said, 'That was way too close.'

'Idiot son?' said Sergeant Zander.

'It worked, didn't it?'

'Jasper said corruption was bad in Estovia,' said Sergeant Zander. 'But is it this bad? Is every official shaking down their citizens?'

'Worse,' said Crutch. 'Jasper told us there's factions in the army, navy, their secret police, the komitav, the city watch, everyone. In Teevilgrad, they all want their cut, and they all have alliances with the top officials in the government.'

'By the gods.'

'Then there's the black market, the unsanctioned slave market. Everyone is working one hustle or another to survive. Even the local bakers are putting sawdust in their bread.'

'It's like a den of thieves.'

'Worse,' said Crutch. 'In a den of thieves, you know who's in charge. In Teevilgrad, it could be anyone who's getting a cut of the action.'

Chapter 12
We Need A Bigger Boat

The Auld Faithful made it to Kodil Bay a couple of hours before sunset. The bay was a four-hour walk from Teevilgrad and was used by the city to quarantine ships with sick crew on board. Cedric had the crew raise a red flag up the mast. A red flag signalled the death grip, a highly infectious disease that made you cough your lungs out. It meant don't come anywhere near this ship. No contact of any kind for forty days.

Crutch and the marines had forty days to get to Teevilgrad, get the glowstone, and get back. They had several sacks of rublets, a significant fortune, sacks full of spear heads, hard tack, bluefire, and some gear.

At midnight, Crutch and the marines slipped into a longboat with all their sacks and rowed silently for the wide river that led into the bay. The town on the shore was quiet, with a single lantern in the watchhouse on the shore. They crouched down as low as they could in the longboat and prayed no one noticed them.

Once they were out of earshot of the town, Boulder took over the rowing, and they went upriver. There were no houses here. The Estovians placed the quarantine zone in the bay because the area was mostly mangroves and dense scrub. As they got further upriver, there was a thump on the hull of the boat.

'What was that?' said Sergeant Zander.

There was a second thump, and the boat rocked hard. Crutch looked in the water and saw a large, dark brown body disappearing under the water.

'Croc,' said Crutch. 'Fifteen feet long, maybe bigger.'

'Shit,' said Sergeant Zander.

Crutch knew it would circle underwater and come back. It would just be a matter of time before it capsized the boat, throwing them all in the water. Worse, if there was one crocodile, there'd be others. Getting thrown into the water here could put them in the water with half a dozen crocs all looking for a feed.

'Quicksilver, give us some light,' said Sergeant Zander.

Quicksilver lit a torch. They scanned the water, but it was still, the only movement on the surface a gentle river's current going out to the sea.

'Where is it?'

Crutch saw it first. Two red eyes reflected in the torchlight coming out of the dark on top of the water.

'There it is.'

It came straight for the side of the boat at full speed. It was bigger than Crutch thought, at least twenty feet long.

'It's a fucking monster,' said Sergeant Zander.

Crutch had his walking cane ready with the blade out. Sergeant Zander had a dagger. Quicksilver held his torch between the boat and the crocodile, hoping the flames might scare it off. The light just seemed to encourage it to swim faster.

The croc hit the side of the boat at full speed, splitting the timber in the top of the hull. Boulder jumped back just in time to avoid its jaws. Crutch looked right into its eyes as it began to move its head so it could get a hold of his body. One bite from that monster would rip him in half.

Crutch drove the blade of his cane, aiming right between the croc's eyes. But the croc had moved its head just before he struck, and the blade slipped off the top of its hard skull without making a scratch.

Sergeant Zander jumped on the back of the croc and pushed its jaws closed with his hands. Crutch knew the croc would roll violently to get him off, and that would smash the boat and Sergeant Zander to pieces.

'Kill it!' yelled Sergeant Zander.

Crutch stabbed at the croc's head again. Again the blade slipped off without making a mark as the croc thrashed its head around. The head of the croc smacked into Crutch's hip, the teeth of the closed mouth cutting into him. It was about to roll. One roll, and they'd all be in the water.

'Stab it between the eyes!' yelled Sergeant Zander.

'I'm trying!'

Crutch held the blade of his walking cane between the croc's eyes, held it there hard while the croc's head shook then pushed down with every ounce of strength he had. The blade ground into the croc's head deep, and the croc stopped moving.

Sergeant Zander rolled off the body of the croc, Boulder and Crutch pushed it back, and it slid into the water. As soon as it went, water started spilling through the crack it had made in the top of the hull.

'Row for the bank,' said Sergeant Zander. 'Now!'

Boulder heaved on the oars. The boat moved painfully slowly as it filled with water. Crutch kept scanning the river around them. The splashing their fight with the first croc had made would attract other crocs.

Sergeant Zander pointed to a muddy clearing in the mangroves. 'We'll go up there.'

By the time they made it to the muddy bank, the longboat was half submerged. Boulder pulled on the oars with enormous force just to keep it moving through the water at a slow crawl. They hit the bank.

'You go first, Crutch,' said Sergeant Zander.

Crutch went off the bow of the boat, jumped down to the bank, and went waist-deep into the mud. He looked behind him, and to his right there was another croc, at least fifteen feet, coming out of the water at speed, heading straight for him.

Crutch tried to move, but he was stuck; the mud sucked at his legs and lower body. When he moved, it just pushed him down further. The croc came at him with its jaws open wide. He could see the rows of teeth, imagined that huge mouth clamping down on his body.

And Boulder jumped on the back of the croc and drove his dagger into its head. The croc's momentum pushed it into Crutch's back with a force that knocked the wind out of him.

'I stabbed it between the eyes,' said Boulder, lying on top of the croc. 'Are you okay Crutch?'

Crutch tried to catch his breath. 'I'm okay.' He prodded the ground ahead of him with his walking cane to find harder ground. 'If you jump up there, the ground should be solid enough to walk on.'

Sergeant Zander and the marines threw their gear off the boat and jumped out onto solid ground. Then they pulled Crutch out of the mud. They looked at the boat, half filled with water.

'Can't use that again,' said Crutch.

'Let's cover it with branches so no one finds it,' said Sergeant Zander. 'Don't need to be setting off red flags for any Estovians who come this way.'

Once they'd covered the longboat, they changed into a clean set of clothes, and Crutch touched up his disguise. They loaded themselves up to walk. Each of them was loaded with sacks full of rublets, spear heads, hard tack, bluefire, oil, and the other equipment they were likely to need. The weight of it all made Crutch's back hurt, and his arm with the walking cane strained every time he moved on it.

They found the road and headed for Teevilgrad. As they walked, Crutch started thinking about how they'd get back to the Auld Faithful. Sergeant Zander must have been thinking the same thing.

'We'll need more than a longboat coming back anyway,' said Sergeant Zander. 'If we're coming with a load of glowstone.'

Crutch nodded. They'd also have to find a way to get the glowstone to the bay. If there was a lot of it, that might be a serious challenge.

'We'll need a bigger boat.'

'A much bigger boat,' said Boulder.

Chapter 13
Teevilgrad City Gates

After four hours walking, Crutch got his first view of Teevilgrad as the first light of dawn started breaking. The city was enormous, with a high wall surrounding it except for the docks. At the rear of the buildings, which were built on a hill, was a large domed building with a gold-painted roof. Below the roof were battlements lined with guards.

'Igor's palace,' said Sergeant Zander. 'From here on, we talk in whispers if we talk at all.'

'We need to find another road in,' whispered Crutch. 'The guards might be suspicious of anyone coming from Kodil Bay. They probably get people trying to escape quarantine.'

Sergeant Zander nodded. Crutch and Sergeant Zander climbed a tree to get a better look at the landscape around them. Past the forest on the side of the road they were on was farmland and a road that led through it to the city gates. That looked like their safest route.

They walked through the forest until they could see the road.

'We should bury some of our supplies, weapons, and coin here,' said Sergeant Zander. 'Trying to get through the city gates with sacks full of spearheads, bluefire, and gold rublets is likely to get us a date with the local torturer.'

Crutch immediately thought about Colonel Romanov from the Zanithburg komitav and how he tortured Sergeant Zander and Quicksilver in front of the crew of the Auld Faithful and cut off

Quicksilver's ear. More torture in an Estovian prison was something they all wanted to avoid.

'If they're having food shortage problems, even the sacks of hard tack could bring attention we don't need,' said Crutch.

They buried most of their gear, including six large sacks of gold rublets. Jasper had fought for them and insisted the navy office give them a small fortune in Estovian currency. Jasper said they caved when he explained to them how much the glowstone was worth to Ironbay and how much it would cost Ironbay if they didn't get it out of Teevilgrad.

The marines carried two weeks worth of hard tack, and Crutch hid several hundred rublets on his body. Hopefully, they wouldn't search him.

Then they crept as close to the road as they could get. They waited for a break in the line of people and carts moving along the road and then walked into the road, heading for the Teevilgrad city gates.

At the city gates, two watchmen questioned everyone before allowing them entry. Crutch went to the front, hobbling forward with his back hunched over.

'What is your business in Teevilgrad?' said the thinner of the two watchmen.

'I am merchant, here to buy goods.'

'And your companions?'

'They help me carry goods. I am old man. Need help.'

'Come with me.' The watchman waved his hand, and two more guards came out of a watch house and helped to escort the marines into a room made of stone blocks with a cell at the back.

'You tell me real reason for visit to Teevilgrad,' said the watchman.

'I tell you real reason. I am merchant, here to buy goods.'

'Can you prove this?'

Crutch tried to think. Was this another shakedown, or was this guard a patriot? If he tried to bribe a patriot, that would land them in jail. If he was trying to shake them down and he didn't offer a bribe, that would land them in jail too. Then he thought about the tariff papers he still had from Inspector Petrov.

'I have border patrol papers from last shipment.' He pulled them out and gave them to the watchman. 'Would not have if I weren't merchant.'

The watchman looked at the papers for a long minute. Then he turned to one of the watchmen, whispered something, and the other watchman left.

'I am watchman Lebedev. I place you in cell. You wait.'

Lebedev locked them in the iron-barred cell at the back of the room and left.

'What is going on?' whispered Sergeant Zander.

'I don't know,' whispered Crutch. 'If I try to bribe him and he's a patriot, we're sunk. If I don't try to bribe him and he wants a bribe, we're sunk too.'

'Should we break out and make a run for it?'

'Then what? They'll be searching the city for us. We'd have to hide, making it impossible to get to our asset, or the glowstone.'

'So we wait?'

'Don't have a choice, do we?'

'This is not going the way we planned. We haven't even got inside the city, and we're already in a prison cell.'

Fifteen minutes later, they could hear the watchman outside.

'Says he is merchant. Sounds fishy, but saw your name.'

The watchman walked in with Inspector Petrov. Petrov smiled.

'Crujge. Didn't think I'd see you so soon.'

'Is lucky coincidence,' said Crutch. 'Watchman Lebedev doing his duty.'

'So you know these men,' said Lebedev.

'Yes. I inspected Crujge's ship. He is merchant like he says.'

'Apologies,' said Lebedev to Crutch, unlocking the cell. 'Must check all new visitors to city with war on. Never know who is Ironworm in disguise.'

'Not Crujge,' said Petrov. 'He is true compatriot.'

Crutch nodded. 'Thank you, Inspector Petrov. You talk true. Liberty for all.'

'Liberty for all,' said Petrov and Lebedev in unison.

Watchman Lebedev escorted them out of the room and onto the road into the city. Inspector Petrov came with them.

'Lucky you have friend in high place,' said Petrov. 'They torture suspicious people who enter city now.'

'Thank you, Inspector Petrov,' said Crutch, then coughed a little. A nice, raspy throat cough for effect. 'I wouldn't survive prison.'

'No, you wouldn't,' said Petrov, smiling.

There was a long pause as Petrov smiled at him, then Crutch realised what was going on.

'How much?' said Crutch.

'How much is freedom worth?' said Petrov, smiling. 'How much is life worth?'

Crutch sighed. 'I give you fifty rublets,' said Crutch. 'And my thanks for saving life.'

'Is good price for your life, but there are five of you.'

'True but idiot son I would be better without. Other companions, not much better. Still I appreciate help. Sixty rublets?'

'That's very generous.'

Crutch looked around. People were walking past them, milling around. 'I give to you here in open?'

'Why not? I told you. I have friends in high place.'

Crutch tried not to look surprised. The corruption here must be at a level beyond extreme if an official was happy to take a bribe in the open on a busy city street.

'Will I have to pay every time I come through gates?' Crutch thought about getting the money, food, and weapons they buried.

'No,' said Petrov. 'Now they know you. Know you are my friend, and tariffs are paid. You and your friends can come and go freely.'

'Thank you,' said Crutch. He counted out the coins and gave them to Petrov. 'Liberty for all,' he said.

'Indeed,' said Petrov, smiling. 'Liberty for all.' Petrov turned and headed out the city gates back towards the docks.

Chapter 14
Without Hope

Crutch and the marines walked deeper into the city. After Petrov's smiling face, the contrast was confronting. The people here had a hollow look in their eyes, like every ounce of hope was sucked from their souls. And they were guarded. They did not make eye contact. Even if you bumped into someone, they'd glance up, go around you, then look down at the ground again.

Many of the people here were thin to the point of emaciation. They had hollow cheeks, and their drab, ragged clothes hung off their bodies.

'They're starving,' whispered Sergeant Zander.

'That should make our task much easier,' whispered Crutch. 'Starving people will do anything to eat.' Crutch knew that better than anyone.

Crutch pulled them into a side alley so he could check the map Jasper gave him of the city. 'The person we need to meet is here,' whispered Crutch, pointing at the map.

'What's that big building two blocks from there?'

'The Teevilgrad komitav operative.'

'Estovia's secret police?'

'Yes.'

'By the gods.'

'Keep your voice down.'

'Our asset works there,' whispered Crutch.

'He's part of the komitav? The secret police?'

'Jasper says they've been working on this asset for years.'

'And if he's really a Solokov patriot?'
'We'll know that fairly quick.'
'How?'
'We'll be dead.'
'At least it'll be quick.'
'Unless they torture us.'
'We can't all turn up to see him at the same time. Before we make contact, we need to find a place to hold up.'
'Somewhere close to where he lives.'
'Because you can never stay too close to the komitav,' said Sergeant Zander.

Finding accommodation was a slow process because they could only move as fast as Crutch could hobble while pretending to be an old man. The inns they found were eager to rent rooms. With starvation and poverty now the norm, they treated anyone who had money to spend like a king.

Their problem was finding a room that didn't have rooms on both sides and thin walls. Crutch and the marines were getting frustrated.

'This is taking too long,' whispered Sergeant Zander. 'The more contact we have with these Estovians, the higher our chance of making a mistake or attracting attention we don't want.'

Crutch knew he was right, but they might be here for four weeks. 'You're right, but staying here four weeks in a room where people can listen in on our conversations is even more dangerous.'

Sergeant Zander nodded.

They went to two more inns with tiny rooms and walls that looked like they were made of paper. Then they got lucky.

'Good day,' said Crutch to the innkeeper behind the bar. The innkeeper was so thin that his clothes barely touched his body. The innkeeper looked Crutch up and down.

'Good day. A drink?'

'Maybe later. Now we look for room. Have rublets.'

The inkeeper's mood improved. He almost smiled, which seemed quite the accomplishment for anyone in Teevilgrad.

'We have plenty good rooms. For all of you?'

'Yes. Looking for something special. A room that is quiet. No rooms next door to it.'

The innkeeper thought for a second then said, 'I have perfect room for you.'

He took them through a solid, locked door at the back of the inn that led down a set of stairs to another solid door. He unlocked that door and led them into a large basement. The basement walls were made of solid stones mortared together. The room was stacked with empty barrels, crates, and half a dozen old bed frames and mattresses.

'We use this room for extra storage of food and ale. Not much food in Teevilgrad, so room is empty. I can clean up for you. Only take an hour or two.'

Crutch hobbled across the room, where he found a door that had a solid bar across it to prevent entry. 'What is on other side of door?' said Crutch.

'Stairs go up to back alley,' said the innkeeper. 'I show you.' He pulled off the solid bar, struggling with its weight, then unlocked the door.

Crutch peered out the door and up the stairs. He hobbled up the steps far enough to see the alley was a dead end, only used by the inn and one building on the other side. They could come and go at any time without being noticed.

He looked back at the other door they came through. It had a heavy bar on the inside to secure it as well.

'Is good,' said Crutch, turning back to the innkeeper. 'Sometimes we load ship all night. Come back to sleep. Don't like to be disturbed. Is this okay?'

'No problem at all. I won't let anyone in.'

'Also, I am merchant. Don't like people come in my room at all. We clean room ourselves. No maids. No light fingers.'

'I understand. I give you only keys to doors. No one will come in. You safe here.'

'Am always safe,' said Crutch. My men are workers and trained fighters. Kill anyone try to steal from me. You understand what I say?'

'I understand,' said the innkeeper. 'I am honest man. Only person working here now since war start. Will not come down here.

'I am happy you honest man. Better honest than dead. Sorry for explanation. Some men not so honest like you.'

'Is okay. You want me to clean out room?'

'No we do ourselves. How much for room?'

The innkeeper looked like he was about to push out a turd, he was so nervous. 'Two rublets a week.'

Crutch almost laughed. He knew that was the innkeeper's first offer, and he'd take much less, but it was next to nothing compared to what he'd already paid in bribes to Inspector Petrov. Best to make the innkeeper happy.

'I pay you two months now. If we left alone to sleep and no one ever disturb us, I give you big tip at end.'

'Really?'

'Yes. I like to reward honest business owner and compatriot. I am honest business owner too. Know how hard business can be in these times.'

Crutch thought the innkeeper would burst into tears when Crutch counted out sixteen rublets. He gave Crutch the keys to both doors and showed him his keyring.

'Those are only keys to this room.'

'Is good,' said Crutch. 'One more thing.'

'Anything.'

'You must not talk of us at all to anyone. Don't mention money you got. Nothing. I am honest merchant, but others not so honest. Try to rob us or steal from us.'

'I understand,' said the innkeeper. 'No one will know you're here.'

'Perfect,' said Crutch.

When the innkeeper left, the marines closed, locked, and barred the door behind him and huddled together in the middle of the room.

'Nice work, Crutch,' whispered Sergeant Zander. 'You didn't even tell him your name.'

'The less he knows, the less he can tell,' whispered Crutch.

'The empty crates and barrels might come in handy,' whispered Quicksilver. 'Wood always burns well.'

'No fire,' whispered Sergeant Zander. 'At least not yet.'

'We can use them for target practice,' whispered Longshot.

'And then the innkeeper wonders why he can hear arrows being shot in his basement,' whispered Sergeant Zander. 'We need to stay invisible.'

'Okay Sarge.'

'Now I can make first contact with our asset,' whispered Crutch.

'The Komitav officer,' whispered Sergeant Zander.

'You didn't have to remind me of that.'

Boulder leaned in and whispered, 'I'm a pumpkin.'

Chapter 15

Family

Crutch stood outside, looking up at a wooden building four stories high, made of timber. Each story had a dozen wooden doors spaced about twelve feet apart. This was where Teevilgrad housed its Komitav and their families.

Crutch checked the directions on the piece of paper Jasper had given him. Third floor, third door on the right at the top of the stairs. He started hobbling his way up the two staircases that would get him there, hunched over, coughing like his lungs could give out at any second.

When he got closer, he played up the clomping of his walking cane. Clomp, step, clomp, step. Someone opened a curtain in one of the rooms and peered out through their wood-barred window. He must have looked a pitiful sight struggling up those stairs.

When he made it to the door on the third floor, he put his weight on his cane with one hand and knocked with the other. A thin man opened the door. The room inside was so small he could see all of it from the doorway. There was a bed, two chairs, a piss bucket, and a tiny area made of stones for cooking with a small chimney. Sitting on the bed was a thin woman, cradling a baby in her arms.

The man looked Crutch up and down. 'Yes?'

'Sorry for interruption. I have unusual question for you.'

'Mmm.'

'Was your grandfather Mikhail Ivenko?'

'Why do you ask?'

Crutch expected that. No one in the Komitav would volunteer information if they didn't have to.

'I know is strange question. Mikhail Ivenko was my father. He had affair with my mother. If he was your grandfather, you are my nephew.' Crutch coughed feebly and wobbled on his legs.

'I'm Anton Ivenko. Come inside and sit down, old man.' Anton grabbed Crutch's arm and led him to a chair.

'Thank you. You very kind.' He made a couple more feeble coughs as the woman holding the baby stared at him. He stared back with as much kindness as he could.

'This is my wife Yelena and my son Nikolai.'

'Your wife and son beautiful. Brings back memories.' Crutch squeezed out a tear. 'So sorry.'

'You say I'm your nephew?' said Anton, sitting in the other chair.

'Is long story. Your grandfather met my mother when he was on ship in port. They had... relations, and I was born. Your grandfather Mikhail Ivenko never came back. Killed in war.'

'Yes he was.'

'Sorry,' Crutch squeezed out another tear. 'Is hard for me. I have wife and daughter like yours when I was younger. They died from the grip. Now I have no one.'

Yelena looked at Crutch with pity in her eyes. 'Would you like to hold him?'

'Could I?'

'Of course.' Yelena carefully placed the baby boy in his arms.

Crutch looked down at the smiling face. The innocence of youth. This baby boy didn't know yet that he was born to poverty. Born to grind and scrape out a living. His only tasks were to suck on his mother's breast, sleep, and smile happily, like he was doing to Crutch right now.

'He's beautiful,' said Crutch, and he meant it. He smiled back at the boy and tickled his tummy. He looked up and saw a kind smile on Yelena's face.

'So sorry. I have not introduced myself. I am Sergey Crujge. Everyone calls me Crujge.' He let out a feeble cough.

'So why come see me now?'

'I only find out about father's other wife in last year. Then I search to see if he had children. When I heard about you, I was so happy. Never expect wonderful surprise like Nikolai.' Crutch smiled again at the baby boy. 'I am so happy.'

'I'm glad you found us,' said Yelena. 'Family is important.'

'Yes. You are good wife. Family is everything. All my family is dead.' Crutch squeezed out another tear. He looked up at Anton.

A tear ran down Anton's cheek. 'All my family is dead too. Now I have just Yelena and Nikolai.'

'And me. If you want,' said Crutch.

Chapter 16
Two Urchins

Hobbling back to the inn, Crutch saw something move out of the corner of his eye down an alley. He looked, and there was a street urchin pulling up a sewer grating. In seconds, Crutch was back in the sewers of Ironbay, that gnawing feeling of hunger in his belly, the constant fear of being caught or beaten, and the endless grind to get something, anything, to eat.

Crutch hobbled down towards the boy and called, 'Boy.'

The street urchin looked up at him coming, pulled the grating over as fast as he could, climbed down the ladder, and disappeared.

'Boy, is alright. I mean you no harm. Want to help you.' Crutch felt in his pocket. He'd love to give the boy a gold rublet, even two or three. That would make a huge difference to any street urchin, but having a gold coin could get him killed. And spending it might be even more of a problem. Shopkeepers would assume he'd stolen it. Crutch pulled out a couple of pieces of silver.

'No one helps street urchins,' called the boy. 'Try to come down here; I stick you.'

'I won't come down. Just want to give you piece of silver. I stay right here. Far enough away, you can run away easy.'

'Don't trust you.'

'I know,' said Crutch. 'I was street urchin just like you. Don't trust anyone. Is smart.'

'You were street urchin?'

'Yes. I prove. You don't sleep in sewer because big rush of water drown you or wash you away. Have to find quiet alley. You go into sewer to escape, to move so no one notice you.'

The boy appeared below the grate. 'You have piece of silver?'

'I have two,' said Crutch.

'Why you give me money?'

'I told you. I was street urchin. Know how hard it is. Just want to help. Make old man happy.'

'No tricks?'

'No tricks. I am old man.'

The boy climbed up and pushed the grate aside. He looked at Crutch with fear in his eyes. Crutch knew that fear. When you lived on the street, it never left you. If it did, you were dead.

'Is okay,' said Crutch. 'I have pieces of silver.

The boy came to him. 'You want something?'

'Just talk. I give you one piece of silver. You sit here, talk to me, then I give you another.' Crutch held the first piece of silver with his arm out, and his palm open.

The boy looked into his eyes, down at the piece of silver. Then he darted forward, grabbed the coin out of his hand, and cowered back, trembling like a dog that had been beaten one too many times by its owner.

'Is okay. I won't hurt you. What is your name?'

The boy stayed in a trembling ball. 'Pavee.'

'Is hard to trust anyone. I understand. Come sit here, and we will talk.' He tapped the ground next to him with his hand. 'I have food.' Crutch always carried a day's worth of hard tack everywhere he went. When you've been a street urchin, carrying food becomes a habit you never break. He pulled out a piece and held it out.

'No tricks?'

'No tricks. Just hate to see you hungry. I know how it feels.'

The boy came up and took the piece of hard tack, still keeping his distance.

'Another piece if you sit, Pavee. Is okay. I am friend.'

One thing Crutch knew from experience. Food had a strange effect on people. When you eat, you feel safer, and the more you eat the safer you feel. With some food in his belly and a silver piece in his pocket, Pavee relaxed enough to sit next to Crutch. Crutch gave him another piece of hard tack.

'You are smart boy to be careful,' said Crutch. 'Living on street is dangerous.'

Pavee kept chewing on the hard tack. From up close, it was obvious to Crutch that Pavee was starving. His cheeks were hollow. Through the holes in his ragged clothes, he could see the bones of his body barely covered by thin skin.

'How old are you?'

'Twelve.'

'What happened to your ma and pa?'

'They died two years ago. Pa died in army. Ma very unhappy, got sick after that. Then she died too.'

'I'm sorry. You been on street since then?'

'Yes.'

'Is hard, but you are strong. You will make it.'

'I get lonely,' said Pavee. 'And scared.'

'I know,' said Crutch. He reached out to put his arm around Pavee. Pavee flinched at the first touch, then relaxed.

'Now there is no food,' said Pavee. He leaned into Crutch and began to sob.

Crutch reached into his pocket and brought out the rest of the hard tack. 'Here is some more.'

Pavee took it, looking at Crutch, his eyes filled with tears. Between his sobs, he said, 'Thank you.'

Crutch sat and talked with Pavee for an hour, maybe more. Then he gave Pavee another five silver pieces. All the silver he had on him. 'A boy like you should not go hungry,' he said, thinking back to the kindness the fisherman had shown him in Quayside. 'I will be in Teevilgrad next few weeks. If you're hungry, find me. I give you food.'

Pavee nodded, doubt on his face. Crutch knew that feeling. Life was so horrible on the streets, when something good happened to you, or someone showed you some kindness, you found it hard to believe.

Crutch thought of inviting the boy back to the inn, but Pavee wouldn't trust him enough yet for that, and it would bring attention from the innkeeper and anyone else who saw him coming and going. It broke his heart to leave him on the street, but at least the boy had food and money now.

'See you soon,' said Crutch.

Pavee nodded and disappeared back down the grate into the sewers.

Chapter 17
The Komitav Operative

Crutch and the marines huddled close together in their room in the basement of the inn, talking softly.

'One thing that might disappoint you,' said Crutch. 'You can't be my idiot son any more.'

'I was just starting to get used to it,' said Sergeant Zander.

'Unfortunately, I don't have a son now.'

'So it worked with Anton?'

Crutch knew from his time begging on the streets of Ironbay when he had someone on the hook. This time, it gave him an awful feeling deep in his guts.

'It worked. Seems wrong, though. He's a good man. His wife is a good person too.'

'In war, we do things we'd never do otherwise,' said Sergeant Zander.

'Just doesn't feel right.'

'If he's in the komitav, he'll have some blood on his hands, good man or not,' said Sergeant Zander. 'And if we handle this just right, he might not get hurt.'

'That's something to hope for, at least,' said Crutch.

'When do we get to burn the city down?'

'Patience Quicksilver,' said Sergeant Zander. 'You'll get your chance. We have a whole pile of other things to set up first.'

'The first thing we need to do is find out where the komitav keep their vault,' said Crutch.

'How are we gonna do that?' said Quicksilver. 'We can't just walk in there asking, 'Do you komitav have a bloody great vault in here somewhere?''

'I guess we'll have to see if we can get a look inside,' said Sergeant Zander. 'Maybe sneak in at night, through the roof, maybe.'

'If they're secret police, it's likely there are guards everywhere. And for the glowstone, you'd expect even more guards.'

'That's not very encouraging,' said Longshot.

'We've overcome much worse problems,' said Sergeant Zander. 'We're marines. We always find a way.'

'Are you all okay?,' said Crutch. 'It can't be easy being stuck in this basement most of the day.'

'We've been in much worse places for much longer. We were stuck in that tiny room in Quayside with nothing but a piss bucket for two months. Until you came along.'

'You brought us soup,' said Boulder.

'Then there was Zanithburg,' said Longshot. 'I've never looked at cockroaches the same way again.'

'We've been using the time to practice our Estovian accents by going up the stairs and listening to the other guests in the inn when they get close to the door.'

'Really?'

'Of course. Listen to this,' said Sergeant Zander. 'Is good day, compatriot. Liberty for all.'

'That's not terrible,' said Crutch.

'It's a work in progress.'

'Have you been practicing too, Boulder?'

'I'm a pumpkin,' said Boulder.

'The Komitav Operative building,' whispered Crutch. 'Jasper told us the vault with the glowstone is in there.'

Crutch was with Sergeant Zander on a roof across from the huge, sprawling komitav building.

'But where?' whispered Sergeant Zander. 'We can't go in there to take a look.'

'Too many guards to try peeking through windows or doors too.' Crutch could see komitav guards in black uniforms with red sashes on almost every door.

'We could try capturing a guard and interrogating him to tell us where the glowstone is,' whispered Sergeant Zander.

'We could. If we did that, we couldn't let the guard go afterwards.'

'No,' whispered Sergeant Zander. 'He'd talk, and then the whole building would be on alert. We'd have to kill him.'

'They have a guard go missing that might put the whole building on alert too.'

'I can't see any guards on the roof,' whispered Sergeant Zander. 'We could get up there and see if we can get in that way.'

'Sounds like as good a plan as any at the moment. Maybe we should get a look from another angle before we go climbing on the roof, though. Don't want any surprises.'

They crawled off the roof they were on and crept through the streets and alleys of Teevilgrad until they got close to the side of the Komitav Operative building. Then they climbed up to the roof of the highest building they could find that was close by.

'No guards on the roof,' whispered Sergeant Zander.

'No guards,' said Crutch, but look at that fenced area between the buildings. Are those what I think they are?'

'Dogs,' whispered Sergeant Zander. 'Bloody guard dogs. Great.'

'Have you ever dealt with a kennel full of guard dogs before Sarge?'

'Once.'

'How did that go?'

'Not well. Half of us got bit. I couldn't walk properly for a week.'

'A dog bit you on the leg?'

'No. I ran across a courtyard with a guard dog chasing me and made it to a fence. I climbed up and thought I was gonna make it out clean.'

'What happened?'

'The bloody dog jumped up and bit me on the arse.'

Crutch tried not to laugh.

'Then it wouldn't let go. It growled and munched on my rear end while I hit it over the head. It shook its head so hard, my sword was ripped off and fell to the courtyard. I punched at it with my fists, but every time I punched it, it just bit down harder, grinding away on the flesh of my arse like it was a doggy snack those nobles give their golden poodles.'

'Didn't you have a dagger?'

'I was just a young marine recruit back then. I didn't carry a belt full of daggers with me.'

'Can't have too many daggers,' whispered Crutch.

'I was the one who taught you that,' said Sergeant Zander. 'Now you know the price I paid to learn it.'

Crutch looked at the kennel and its stone yard. 'Is that a drainage grate in the yard?'

'I think it is,' whispered Sergeant Zander. 'You think we can go through the sewers and get in through there?'

'I doubt it,' said Crutch. 'They'll have it reinforced with bars into the rock. We could get under there to take a better look, though.'

Sergeant Zander and Crutch climbed off the building next to the Komitav Operative, and Crutch found a way into the sewers. After wandering around through the sewerage water, Crutch finally saw the grate over the guard dog's kennel yard.

But as they got closer, the dogs started barking. They couldn't get close enough to look up through the grate without setting the dogs off.

'Best not to work the dogs up,' said Sergeant Zander. 'The komitav guards might start looking in the sewer grate.'

Crutch and Sergeant Zander went back through the sewers to the grate in the alley they'd climbed down, climbed back out, and headed for the inn.

'Dogs,' said Sergeant Zander to the marines in the room in the basement of the inn. 'They've got bloody dogs at the Komitav Operative building.'

'I hate guard dogs,' said Longshot. 'Yapping their heads off when you're trying to sneak around.'

'Gonna make it near impossible to get into the building with the dogs there,' said Sergeant Zander.

'We could set them on fire,' said Quicksilver.

'Maybe,' said Sergeant Zander. 'But do you think a dozen guard dogs running around on fire might attract the kind of attention we want to avoid?'

'Hard to say,' said Quicksilver.

'Killing them's not really an answer anyway,' said Crutch. 'They'll just bring in more dogs.'

'So we need to make them rethink having dogs at all.'

'This would be a whole lot simpler if the komitav were all cat lovers,' said Longshot.

'I might have an idea,' said Crutch.

CHAPTER 18
A MOTHER WHO LOVED HIM

When Crutch got to Anton's building the second time and began climbing the stairs, Anton came running down.

'Let me help you, uncle.' Anton held him under the arm. Crutch let as much weight fall on Anton's arm as he could.

'Thank you, Anton. And thank you for calling me uncle. Is nice.' With Crutch going as slowly and feebly as he could, it took quite some time to get up all the stairs. 'Sorry to take so long. My old bones are weak.'

'Is okay,' said Anton, patiently helping him make each step. 'I don't mind.'

When they reached Anton's room, Yelena came out of the door and wrapped her arms around Crutch in a warm hug.

'Thank you for coming back. Is so good to see you.'

'Thank you for seeing me again,' said Crutch. 'You're very kind.'

'You're welcome any time,' said Yelena, pulling back and looking into his face. 'You're family.'

Crutch felt a surge of warmth inside. They were so kind. Was this what it was like to have a family? To have people who cared for you just because you were their blood?

'Come inside and sit,' said Anton, guiding him through the door into their tiny room. Crutch could see Nikolai sleeping in a cradle made of rough wood next to the two chairs.

Anton helped Crutch into the chair next to Nikolai's cradle and sat in the other chair. Yelena sat at the end of the bed, right next to the cradle. Her gaze shifted from smiling kindly at Crutch to looking down with devotion at her baby Nikolai.

Crutch watched Yelena look at her son and wondered what it might be like to have a mother who loved him like that, like he was the most important thing in her world. Like he was her whole world.

'You are good mother,' said Crutch, his throat so tight his voice cracked a little as he said it.

Yelena looked at Crutch and smiled. 'Thank you.'

'Yelena is best mother any son could have,' said Anton. 'And best wife any husband could have.'

'Oh, stop,' said Yelena, blushing.

'Is true,' said Anton. 'For me, my whole world is you. I live to see your face in morning and when I come home at night.'

Yelena squeezed Anton's hand and put the other hand on his cheek. 'You're my world too. You and Nikolai.' For a second, it was like Crutch wasn't in the room as they looked into each other's eyes. Then Yelena looked at Crutch and said, 'So sorry, Crujge. You don't want to see us making eyes with each other.'

'No. Is beautiful. I have girl once,' said Crutch, thinking of Abagail and her beautiful, crooked face. Then he thought about how she never came to say goodbye at the docks, and a deep pain flooded into his heart like someone had stabbed him in the chest and slowly turned the dagger round and round. 'She's gone now.'

'I am so sorry, uncle,' said Anton. 'Must be hard for you to see people together.'

'Not your fault. Is just hard having lost…' His voice broke as Crutch thought about Abagail again. He pulled himself together and managed a feeble, half-sad smile. 'Is good to see you together. You make me happy.'

'I am happy too,' said Anton. 'I think my whole family dead and now I have uncle. Nice surprise in these hard times.'

'Times very hard. Are you okay?'

'Very hard to buy food. Sometimes Yelena has to line up at store for hours holding baby.'

'Is not right,' said Crutch.

'Then food is expensive,' said Anton. 'Sometimes ten times what it used to be before war.'

'If you can get food at all,' said Yelena. 'Last week I stand in line three hours for yams. Get to front of line, and no yams left.'

'Emperor Solokov says food is stopped by Ironborn warships,' said Anton.

'Is not Ironborn warships,' said Crutch.

'No?'

'I am from Uraskova, where most food for Teevilgrad is grown,' said Crutch. 'Food is short because Estovia forced men into army. Without men, yams, and bananas, and sweet potatoes rot in fields. No one to harvest and no one to plant crops. Is not Ironbay making Teevilgrad hungry. Is Solokov forcing men into army.'

Anton's eyes went wide. 'Speak softly when you talk of these things, uncle. Walls here are thin. Don't know who might listen.'

'I am sorry, Anton. I don't know about hiding in shadows like komitav. I am just simple merchant.'

'Is okay,' said Anton so softly his voice was nearly a whisper. 'Whole of Teevilgrad is hungry. Now I know why. Sometimes Yelena is so hungry her milk dries up. Have to feed Nikolai with sugar and water.'

'Is not right,' said Crutch. 'My family should not starve because of Emperor Solokov. Makes me sad and angry.'

'Some are very angry,' said Anton. 'But must be careful. Solokov will kill anyone who talks bad about him or tries to make change.'

'He kills people who try to do good?'

'Yes.'

Crutch shook his fist. 'Is not right. Not right.' He cut off the last word with hard, deep, raspy coughs.

'Don't work yourself up,' said Yelena. 'You too old to get angry. Leave for young men.'

'That's problem with world,' said Crutch. 'Old men leave problems for young men to fix. Young men go hungry, young men fight in old men's war. Maybe time for old men to change, make world better.' Crutch coughed again. This time weaker, wheezing as he coughed.

'You talk truth,' said Anton, 'but maybe not you. You too old, too sick to fight big fight.'

'You are right,' said Crutch. He put one hand on Anton and another on Yelena. 'You are good people. I am so lucky to have you as family. So happy I found all three of you.' He smiled feebly at Nikolai in his cradle made of old, discarded wood.

'We are happy too,' said Anton. Yelena nodded.

'Maybe there is something I can do,' said Crutch. 'I am blessed with you, and I am blessed in business. As merchant, I have money.' Crutch reached into his pocket and pulled out two rublets. 'I want to give to you.'

'No,' said Anton. 'I can't.'

'I understand,' said Crutch. 'You are good man. You provide for your family. But you're my family too.'

'Is not right,' said Anton.

'Shops being empty of food is not your fault,' said Crutch. 'Food being ten times normal price not your fault. Is Solokov's fault.'

'Is true,' said Anton.

Crutch looked down in his lap. 'I have no one else. Please make an old man happy and take this. Not for you. For Nikolai. No child should go hungry.' When he looked up, Anton and Yelena were crying.

'We will take,' said Anton. 'You are good man.'

'Thank you,' said Yelena, her face wet with tears. 'Thank you so much. You are like angel.'

Crutch was crying too. He didn't have to force out these tears. They were real.

Chapter 19
Give Me Money Or Die

As he headed back to the inn from Anton's room, Crutch noticed someone following him. One thing about hobbling around like an old man was that moving so slowly made it impossible to follow you without sticking out.

Crutch hobbled on, watching the man following him out the side of his eye. Male. Twenties. Thin. But then everyone except Emperor Solokov was thin in Teevilgrad, so it didn't help identify whoever it was. It could be anyone.

What did he want? Were the Komitav on to him? Was Anton playing a brilliant game of deception? Had he already given him up? Only one way to find out.

Crutch hobbled into an alley and gave the man following him his chance. The man was quick and silent. He felt a blade against his back before he even heard a footstep.

'No need to die, old man. Give me your money.'

A simple robbery. If he didn't have a blade at his back, Crutch would have been relieved.

'I give you money,' said Crutch. 'Just let me get.' Crutch turned to get a better view of this robber, brought up his cane, released the blade, and aimed to stab him in the foot while he grabbed the knife with his other hand.

But the robber had moved his foot before the cane got to him. And the robber's hand holding the knife wasn't there either. This guy knew how to fight.

Crutch went to move out of range and face the robber, but before he had a chance, the robber had kicked his walking cane hard. It flew across the alley into a brick wall.

'Not so old then. Still give me money.' He could see the robber now. A thin man in black robes with a hood. The hood shadowed his face. There was no way he could recognise him. It didn't matter now. This robber knew he was not an old man. He had to die, whoever he was. At least he wasn't innocent.

'Give me money,' said the robber again. 'Or die.'

'Come and get it,' said Crutch.

'Die it is then.' The robber advanced with his knife pointed straight at Crutch's eyes. Good technique. With a dagger pointed at your eyes, it was much harder to judge how far it was from you. In the moonlight in a dark alley, it was harder still.

The robber moved slowly, carefully, then he exploded with speed, lunging forward, catching Crutch by surprise, swinging one leg under Crutch's good leg, and knocking him to the ground. The robber followed up with a knife attack, still keeping the knife pointed at Crutch's eyes. Crutch rolled at the last second, and the robber's knife clanked onto the cobblestones of the alley.

Crutch swung his good leg at the robber's knee hard, but before it hit, the robber had gone from crouching on his knee to a swift jump backwards. Crutch knew he was in real trouble. With his cane, this would be a tough opponent. Without it, he would likely end up dead. The reality was, this robber was a better fighter than him.

Crutch crawled towards his cane, still four yards away. The robber anticipated his move and cut off his path. Crutch feinted a move left, then jumped right. The robber saw it coming and cut him off again. Crutch had another problem. He could move on one leg, but it was slow and awkward without his cane.

The robber came in for another attack, again with the knife pointing right at Crutch's eyes. Crutch jumped out of the way towards his cane and started crawling with speed. His hand was just an inch away from the cane when the robber kicked it away. Crutch looked up on all fours at the robber, who had a sad smile.

'Is shame you must die. You good fighter for a cripple.' The robber started thrusting his knife down for that final killing blow.

And looked at Crutch in shock as Crutch moved up and drove his own dagger right into the robber's heart. You can never have too many daggers.

The robber fell to the ground, blood pumping from the wound in his chest. As Crutch knelt at the robber's side, his eyes were already glazed over in death. Crutch checked his pockets to see if he carried anything that might tell him who he was or where he was from. There was nothing.

Maybe just a robber who saw an easy victim in the night. Maybe. Crutch picked up his cane and peered round the corner to make sure the street was empty before hobbling out of the alley.

When he got back to the basement of the inn, he told Sergeant Zander and the marines about the attack.

'So it's true,' said Sergeant Zander.

'What's that?'

'There were stories that the komitav have a secret hand-to-hand fighting technique that's especially deadly.'

'You think he was komitav?'

'Sounds like it,' said Sergeant Zander. 'Young, fit men that age are in the army, navy or komitav. The way he fought sounds like komitav.'

'The one mistake he made was assuming I only had one weapon. I didn't pull the dagger until the very last second. That took him by surprise.'

'It's always the attack you don't see coming,' said Sergeant Zander.

'It was very nearly me who didn't see this robber's attack coming.'

'There's another question,' said Sergeant Zander.

'What's that?'

'Why was a komitav officer trying to rob you?'

'He was skinny. The komitav are starving like everyone else. I found that out tonight with Anton and Yelena. That's one explanation anyway.'

'I hope you're right,' said Sergeant Zander.

'You're worried someone in the komitav is on to us?'

'Yes. I think it's just a matter of time.'

Crutch thought about that. 'Crujge' was a stranger from out of town claiming to be a relative. Someone Anton had never met. Even if Anton trusted him, the place he lived in was full of komitav officers. They had to expect he'd be under some kind of scrutiny.

'We'll have to make some backup plans,' said Crutch. 'Assume they're going to work out I'm not who I say I am.'

'We also need to practice fighting these komitav,' said Sergeant Zander.

'I don't think I can get Anton to give his ageing uncle lessons.'

'No, but we can work with what we know.'

Crutch and the marines worked through every move the robber had used, analysing it and the thinking behind it. They came up with ways to counter each move. To anticipate each move before it came.

And they thought through the fighting method and what other moves someone who fought like that might use. Then they came up with ways to counter those too. Then they practiced for hours.

It was imprecise, and they knew they'd be in trouble fighting any komitav officer, but at least they all had some preparation now.

Chapter 20
The True Compatriots

Anton and Yelena met Crutch outside a massive wooden-floored hall. The hall was run down, now but once it must have been magnificent to behold. It could easily hold thousands of people if they were standing.

'This was community dance hall before war,' said Anton. 'Since war, no one has energy for dancing.'

'I met Anton at dance here,' said Yelena. She held Nikolai in one arm. With the other, she squeezed Anton's hand.

'Best day of my life,' said Anton.

Crutch smiled. 'Is beautiful,' he said, trying not to think about the day he met Abagail. A picture of her in her shimmering pink and silver dress, that wonderful crooked face, and those deep, ocean blue eyes flooded his mind. Abagail standing there, offering the marines pastries and inviting Crutch to her birthday party.

'We call ourselves the True Compatriots,' said Anton. 'Just good people from Teevilgrad. We talk about important things and help each other.'

'Is good,' said Crutch. 'Thank you for inviting me.'

'Remember, don't tell anyone,' said Anton. 'Could be dangerous.'

'I am not clever komitav like you,' said Crutch, 'but I remember.'

As they formed, the True Compatriots sat in a circle of old chairs. They were ordinary people. Women, men, and their children looking sad and starved, sitting on the floor. Anton sat with Yelena on his left, Nikolai sleeping peacefully in her lap. There were forty adults here sitting in two rows, huddled together, talking softly.

'Teevilgrad can be better place. Estovia can be better place,' said Anton. 'Twenty years we have peace with Ironbay; now is war. War means good men die. For what? Instead of making weapons, we can build homes for Estovians. Instead of sending men to war, they can grow food so everyone has plenty.

'My uncle Crujge is from Uraskova. He tells me they forced men there into army. Crops are rotting in ground. Food that would feed everyone in Teevilgrad goes to waste because men die in war that makes no sense. The enemy is not Ironbay. The enemy is our thinking.'

There was murmuring in the group.

One man spoke up from the second row, near Anton.

'Is it true that food is rotting in ground in Uraskova?'

Anton looked at Crutch. 'This is Yevgeny. He is trusted friend many years uncle. Works with me in komitav. All people here I trust. You can speak openly.'

For a komitav officer, Anton seemed quite naive. Trusting another officer of the secret police seemed like an idea that would end badly for everyone involved. But Crutch was in Teevilgrad to get a job done.

'Is true,' said Crutch. I have ship. Transport food from Uraskova to other Estovian islands and territories for many years. Now farmers are desperate. Can't get workers to harvest crops. Can't get workers to plant crops. All young men forced into army or navy. Men older than me working in fields doing hard labour now.'

Gasps of surprise filled the room.

'Is even worse than you told me,' said Anton.

'Is not right,' said Crutch. He knew he walked a tightrope here. Don't say anything that suggests treason or rebellion, even though that's exactly where this group had to go if their plan was to work.

'We need change,' said Anton. 'Need to stop this war and start building again. Is wrong Estovians live in poverty. Is wrong we can't feed children.'

'I am compatriot,' said Crutch. 'Have been compatriot my whole life. Never seen things so bad. Even in last war, twenty-three years ago, Estovians had food. You are right, Anton. We need change.'

'What can we do?'

Crutch knew exactly what they had to do, but he also knew that was a conclusion they would have to reach themselves when their hunger turned to frustration and then anger. Looking at all of them, that time was not far off, but they weren't there yet.

They were still thinking reasonably, like there was a government of leaders who would see reason and find a path through the mess they'd created. But with Emperor Solokov leading the parade, there was no way it would be heading down a side street, no matter how much better that would be for everyone.

'When I was boy, we said victory for all and meant it,' said Crutch. 'Now is victory for none.'

'And we all starve,' said Anton.

'Is not right,' said Crutch, pushing out a raspy cough. 'You good people. Deserve good lives. Is not right.'

After everyone had left, it was just Crutch, Anton, and Yelena carrying Nikolai on her chest.

'Thank you for coming,' said Anton.

'Thank you for inviting me. Is good thing you are doing. Good but dangerous.'

'Is true,' said Anton. 'But we must have change in Teevilgrad. If not, we all starve anyway. Better to stand and die fighting than starve on knees.'

And there it was. Good people fighting and dying in another battle that should never have begun. Good people trying to clean up the mess lesser men made for them.

Crutch looked sadly at Anton and Yelena. 'You are good people. Your friends good people too. Makes me sad you must fight. Maybe die. Too much death already.' His throat went tight as Crutch thought about all the men he'd led to their deaths on the Kona track. Young men with so much hope, so much promise, cut down before their lives had even started.

'You are good man too,' said Yelena, touching his arm.

'Thank you. Maybe not so good. Selfishly made rublets for myself for so many years. Maybe could have done more for others.'

'Don't say this,' said Yelena. 'You have been so kind to us.'

'Your help saved us,' said Anton.

'I want to help more,' said Crutch. 'Help all your friends. Help your cause. Give you money to help.'

'I didn't invite you for money,' said Anton.

'I know you didn't. You do great work here, Anton. Your dream of better Estovia is wonderful. You're great man.' And Crutch meant it. If men like Anton ruled Estovia and Ironbay, maybe there wouldn't be so much pain and so much hunger. Maybe there wouldn't be street urchins trying to survive in the sewers. Maybe they'd have a roof over their heads and food every night. Life was full of dreams and maybes. Maybe just once, one dream could come true.

'Is too much,' said Anton. 'You can't do this.'

'I must do this,' said Crutch. 'Make up for doing nothing all my life. Please let this old man leave this world with some peace.'

Anton looked at Crutch. 'Thank you,' said Anton. 'With money, we can make posters, get more food for people who are starving. We can make big difference.'

'Is good,' said Crutch. 'Next time, I will bring you more rublets. I have idea too. Something that will help people. I need your help for this.'

'What is idea?' said Anton.

'I explain later. Now I am tired. Must go sleep.'

'You should be careful,' said Anton. 'Just two days ago, neighbour in room right next door to me killed in same streets you walk.'

'Really?'

'Yes. You are old man, uncle. Easy prey for robber. Don't want to see you hurt.'

Crutch thought about the tiny room Anton and Yelena lived in. The walls must be thinner than he thought. At least he knew now who had tried to rob him.

'You are good man Anton, to worry about me. I will bring worker next time. He can be bodyguard for this old man.'

Before he left, Yelena hugged him goodbye with one arm, the other holding Nikolai. Up close, Crutch could see some colour had returned to her cheeks. Inside, he felt a surge of happiness that his money had bought her food. Before she pulled away, Crutch held her hand and slipped two rublets into it.

'For Nikolai.'

Yelena smiled, her face close to tears of appreciation. 'Thank you Crujge. You are our angel.'

Chapter 21
The Dogs Will Bark

Crutch led the marines through the sewers, catching rats and cockroaches. They put the rats in a crate they'd turned into a rat cage, and put the cockroaches in jars they found in the basement of the inn they were staying at.

Once they had enough of them, they walked through the sewers until they got close to the grate under the Komitav Operative dog kennel. Crutch looked at the rats and thought it was a shame to waste good food. His mouth watered thinking about what the rats would taste like, cooked up or even raw. It was all he could do not to pull one out of the wooden cage and bite into it right now.

The sacrifices you make when you're a marine. Crutch and Sergeant Zander walked the last twenty feet to the grate under the dog kennel, with Crutch carrying a jar of cockroaches. The dogs started barking as soon as they were within ten feet.

'Better make this quick,' said Sergeant Zander. 'We don't want the komitav guards to look into this grate and see us looking back at them.

Crutch put the jar of cockroaches against the grate while Sergeant Zander held a blanket up, so the only way the cockroaches could go was up into the kennel yard. Crutch opened the top of the jar, and the cockroaches swarmed out of the grate into the kennel, heading for the nearest dark corners and crevices.

The dogs went crazy, chasing after the cockroaches. They ran in wild circles, their barks and whines making a deafening sound. They scratched at the tiny cracks the cockroaches disappeared into, whining and barking. As Crutch and Sergeant Zander retreated back down the sewer tunnel, they could hear the Komitav guards.

'What is wrong with you?'

'Stupid dogs shut up. Is nothing here.'

'Round one to the cockroaches,' whispered Sergeant Zander.

Through the next grate in the alley away from the Komitav Operative building, Crutch saw three cats prowling, making mewing sounds, their tails wagging.

'Think we could catch some of those cats?' whispered Crutch.

'I can catch them,' whispered Longshot. 'I had a cat for years before a big storm washed it off the ship.'

'Longshot crawled out into the alley, pulled some dried fish out of his pocket, and in less than a minute, he had half a dozen cats purring and eating out of his hand while he stroked them and scratched their necks.

'Get them to where they can see the kennel yard,' whispered Crutch.

Longshot nodded and coaxed the cats to the end of the alley with some more dried fish.

Crutch and Sergeant Zander walked back down to the grate under the dog kennel, carrying the rat crate. The dogs started barking as soon as they were within ten feet.

Crutch and Sergeant Zander held the crate up to the grate so there was nowhere for the rats to go but up, and slid off one of the planks. Crutch prodded at them from underneath. The rats saw their chance at freedom and jumped out into the kennel yard, running fast for the walls.

As soon as the rats jumped into the kennel yard, the dogs went completely insane. They were frustrated about not catching the cockroaches, and they didn't want to be beaten again.

Lonshot's cats added to the pandemonium, racing across the road, up the fence and walls, then down into the yard after the rats. That took the dogs' frenzy to another level. The guard dogs were chasing rats and cats, running into the walls and fence of their yard at full speed, then yelping in pain when they hit. They barked, they growled, they spun in circles, fell over onto their sides, and kept right on running.

As Sergeant Zander and Crutch walked back away from the grate again, they heard the komitav guards.

'Is just cat stupid dogs.'

'Shut up!'

Crutch got to the alley so he could watch the fun. The dogs were ignoring the guards, now trying to jump up the walls to get to the cats. One cat jogged away along the top of the wall with a dead rat in its mouth.

'I said shut up!'

'And the rats win round two,' whispered Sergeant Zander.

They had two more jars of cockroaches they released up the grate in the kennel yard, one at a time. Now the cats saw the kennel grate as a source of food, they'd wait near the top of the walls around the kennel for something to come out and race around looking for a chance to get a tasty moving snack.

The cats at the top of the walls drove the dogs crazy, making them bark and whine even when Crutch and Sergeant Zander weren't setting cockroaches free.

'A few more nights of this, and they'll be ready to throw their dogs in the ocean,' whispered Sergeant Zander as they made their way back to the inn after their night of fun.

Chapter 22
Two More Street Urchins

'What will you do with this food?' said Inspector Petrov.

Crutch and Sergeant Zander were on the docks of Teevilgrad, next to Petrov's border patrol ship.

'Feed street urchins and starving people of Teevilgrad,' said Crutch.

'You want me to tell you about shipments of food going to nobles and rich people of Teevilgrad so you can buy?'

'Yes.'

'Then you give food to starving people?'

'Exactly.'

'Makes no sense. What is in this for you?'

'I am old man,' said Crutch. He hacked out a deep, raspy cough. 'Before I die, want to do something good in world. Is like old man's dying wish.'

'Except you do while you still alive?'

'Yes.'

Petrov looked Crutch up and down like he was inspecting a fillet of fish in the street markets. 'Tell me real story.'

'I already tell you real story,' said Crutch. 'I was street urchin myself when little boy. Know what is like to be hungry.'

'You were street urchin?'

'Yes.'

'Prove it.'

'Best place to hide is in sewers. City watch don't want to get shit and piss on boots. You can't sleep in sewers, though. Big rush of water drown you, or wash you away. So you find corner in alley. But not near tavern, or inn, or restaurant. Owners don't like, and will kick you and hit you in middle of night. Don't be brave. Run at first sign of trouble if you want to live.'

Petrov's eyes were wide. 'You talk true. You were street urchin.'

'You only know because you were street urchin too,' said Crutch. 'Know what is like to starve on street, hide in sewers.'

'Yes,' said Petrov. 'I was street urchin for two years after mother died. Then I get job as deck boy on border patrol boat. Best day of my life.'

'I get job cleaning out pig pens on ship. Best day of my life too.'

'We are brothers,' said Petrov. 'Now I feel bad I charge you so much for help.'

Crutch smiled. 'You give rublets back?'

'Don't be ridiculous,' said Petrov, and they both laughed. 'But I help you. Tell you which ships have food you look for. Also, I cut ship's tariff on food so you can buy cheaper.'

'You do this for me?'

'I do this for street urchins and hungry people of Teevilgrad. Also, fuck nobles. They never help when I starve on street. Maybe they find out what is like to be hungry.'

'How much?' said Crutch.

'This I do free.'

'Really?'

'Yes. Where you give out food?'

'Community dance hall near Komitav Operative.'

'Good. I come down and see for myself. If this is trick, you will take fast trip to komitav jail. Is close by.'

'Is no trick.'

'I believe you,' said Petrov. 'Come with me. I introduce you to ship captains.'

Crutch sat in the front seat of the horse and wagon he'd just bought, with Sergeant Zander next to him. The wagon was loaded with crates and barrels full of vegetables, sacks of whiteroot flour, and sugar. Boulder sat in the wagon among the crates he'd just helped load off the ships.

'Explain to me how this is going to help us again,' whispered Sergeant Zander.

'Anton needs a lot more followers if he's going to create the kind of problems we need to get the glowstone out of the Komitav Operative building. To get more followers, he needs people to trust him.'

'So he gives food to people who are hungry?'

'Exactly,' whispered Crutch. 'It's low risk to begin with. It looks like he's running a charity helping street urchins. Then he starts feeding anyone who needs it.'

'And Solokov can't do anything about it. If he does, it brings even more attention to the fact that people are starving under his rule.'

'Either way, Solokov loses. If he does nothing, Anton and the True Compatriots build their following. If he tries to stop the food going to the hungry, the hungry people will rise up against him. At least that's what I hope will happen.'

'You think Solokov will come up with something else?'

'He's the ruler of Estovia for a reason. Best not to underestimate him.'

Boulder helped carry in crates full of vegetables, sacks full of flour and sugar, and barrels of water. Yelena and Anton set up three big cooking pots friends had loaned her. They cut up the vegetables and threw them in water. Once they were cooking, Yelena added some sugar and whiteroot flour.

'We could make bread,' said Yelena, 'but will go much further if we add to soup. Water fills you up. Sugar and flour give you energy.'

'Can add rat and cockroach to fill out too,' said Crutch leaning over the pot. 'Plenty of cockroaches in the sewer.'

Yelena looked at Crutch with her mouth open. Then she started laughing.

'Oh Crujge. I didn't know you were such jokester.'

Crutch didn't understand why she was laughing. He wasn't joking, but he laughed with her to keep from drawing attention to something he might have missed.

Pavee told the local street urchins there was free soup. They were reluctant at first, expecting some kind of trick, but when they saw the other urchins eating, they put aside their fears enough to come in, take a bowl and spoon, and line up to be served.

After a couple of days, there were so many urchins Yelena needed help serving them. Boulder and Crutch stood next to Yelena and ladled out the soup from the three huge cooking pots. The children had some trust now, and they laughed and talked as they ate.

When Crutch was a street urchin, he never dreamed the end to his hunger could be so simple. All it took was a little money and a little kindness.

When Yelena was away from them, stoking the cooking fire, Boulder whispered, 'I gave them soup.'

Crutch smiled and felt like crying with joy as he looked out into the room filled with happy faces. 'Yes, you did,' he whispered. Remember, no talking.'

Boulder grinned, joy on his face too. 'I'm a pumpkin.'

CHAPTER 23

THE KOMITAV OPERATIVE ROOF

'There's no dogs,' said Longshot as the marines huddled together in the inn after Crutch and Boulder got back from the soup kitchen.

'Are you sure?' said Sergeant Zander.

'I'm sure. Quicksilver and me even let some rats loose through the grate in the kennel.'

'The cats ran straight down the walls to catch those rats,' said Quicksilver. 'They weren't worried at all. They knew the dogs weren't there.'

'We don't know if they'll stay gone,' said Sergeant Zander. 'We should check out the Komitav Operative building tonight.'

'You want to break in?' said Crutch.

'We don't know enough to do that safely. I say we check out the roof and see if there's a way in, or at least a way we can spy on what's inside.'

The marines hid near the walls of the alley across from where the dog kennel was. They wore thin black robes covering their heads and their bodies. Crutch still wore his face paint. Taking it all off was too much work and used up too much of the paint. He started with just one large jar of the face paint, and he was already half way through it.

Sergeant Zander had gone through the sewers all the way to the grate under the dog kennel, and there was nothing. No barking, no whining, no growling. No dogs.

'This is still the only stretch of the outside wall without guards,' whispered Sergeant Zander. 'We'll have to climb up this way, just like those cats did.'

'We'll have to be careful,' whispered Crutch. We know there were guards in the building just next to the dog kennel.'

'At the first sign of trouble, we get out of there as fast as we can,' whispered Sergeant Zander. 'We can't let them see Crutch with his walking cane. They might figure out Crujge at the soup kitchen is the same person.'

'I'll crawl while I'm on the roof,' whispered Crutch. I can move faster like that anyway.'

Sergeant Zander nodded his approval.

'Which way should we go if we hit trouble?' whispered Longshot.

'On the roofs until we can get down without being seen, then into the sewers. You all ready?'

Crutch and the other marines nodded.

The marines climbed up two vertical support beams to the roof about fifteen feet up, keeping a watch for guards. The top of the roof was an expanse of roof tiles. Crutch couldn't see a chimney or an air hole anywhere.

'Let's see if there's anything on the other side,' whispered Sergeant Zander.

Crutch crawled, looking at the tiles of the roof under him, hoping he might see something, some way in, anything. But there was nothing. Just roof tiles.

They went over the high point of the building to the other side, and it was the same. No chimneys, no way to get in.

'They mustn't cook in the building,' whispered Sergeant Zander.

'How are we gonna get in?' whispered Longshot.

'Maybe we can pull off a few of these tiles and make a hole big enough that we can get in that way,' whispered Quicksilver.

Quicksilver pulled at a tile, and it wouldn't budge. He tried pulling harder, his face straining. Still nothing. He took a dagger out of his belt, slipped it under the tile, and moved it around until it caught on something.

'That's it,' he whispered. He pushed the dagger forward, smiled, then pulled the handle up as hard as he could. The tile shot up in the air, landed back on the roof, and started sliding for the edge.

Longshot dove after it as it slid, his own body sliding towards the edge. The tile slipped over the edge, and Longshot went with it, grabbing the tile in midair, his own body now over the edge of the roof and about to fall.

Boulder grabbed his ankle at the last second and pulled him back up. Crutch heard a whistle blow.

'People on roof!' yelled a guard.

'Time to go,' whispered Sergeant Zander.

They went back the way they came across the tiles and over the high point of the roof.

Crutch crawled across the roof at full speed, the marines running right beside him. Crutch could see the edge of the roof up ahead.

'We don't have time to climb down,' whispered Sergeant Zander. 'They'll be on to us before we get to the ground. We'll have to jump to the roof of the next building.'

The other marines sped up to a sprint before leaping across to the roof of the next building. Crutch went last, crawling as fast as he could, then pushing off with all his strength using his good leg.

He realised as he saw the other building coming that he hadn't jumped far enough. He reached out with both his hands, but his fingertips were just a few inches short. He was about to fall fifteen feet to the cobblestone street below.

Boulder caught his left arm with both hands, and Sergeant Zander caught his right arm. His body slammed into the wall below the roof before Boulder and Sergeant Zander hauled him up.

'Keep going,' whispered Sergeant Zander as Crutch caught his breath. 'Don't let them see us.'

When they got to the other side of the roof, Crutch could see an alley off the main street. The alley had a sewer grate.

'We can hide in the sewers there,' he whispered.

'Good thinking,' whispered Sergeant Zander.

They half climbed, half slipped down the vertical support beams of the building. Sergeant Zander led them down the alley, pulled off the grate, and jumped down into the sewer. Boulder,

Longshot, and Quicksilver followed them. Crutch was about to jump down.

'I can't go any further,' whispered Quicksilver.

'What?' whispered Longshot.

'I can't go any further. The sewer here goes into a pipe that a cat would have trouble getting through.'

'I'm halfway under the grate,' whispered Quicksilver. 'And Crutch isn't even in yet. They'll see us if they walk over the grate.'

It was already too late. Crutch could see komitav officers heading along the main street, going down each alley. Their alley was next. Crutch threw his robe down the sewer and slid the grate back on. 'Stay here,' he whispered.

Crutch moved as quick as he could until he was at the end of the alley, then he started hobbling.

'Over here!' yelled one komitav officer. Six others quickly surrounded him, their weapons drawn. Their leader came walking up with a purpose.

'He was alone coming out of the alley, Arch Warden Gragor,' said one of the officers.

'What you doing here this late?' said Arch Warden Gragor.

'Working at soup kitchen. Had to help street urchin.'

'Tell truth,' said Gragor. 'You Ironworm spy.'

'Am just simple merchant. Help out poor urchins in street who have no food, no place to live.'

This was going badly. Crutch knew he was one interrogation from spending the rest of a very short life in the komitav jail. If they stripped him of his clothes, they'd quickly discover he wasn't an old man.

'We get truth from you, said Gragor. 'Take him to Komitav Operative. If you are spy, it will be bad. Very bad.'

More komitav officers ran up the street towards him.

'Wait!' yelled one of the officers. It was Anton, breathing hard from running. 'Arch Warden Gragor, please wait. This is my uncle.'

Gragor looked at Anton. 'Your uncle?'

'Yes. He is merchant. Helps Yelena run soup kitchen for street urchins. Gives money to poor. Is good man.'

'I try to tell them this,' said Crutch, coughing. He pushed out a tear. 'They want to send me to komitav. I am old man. Just simple merchant. Sorry if I do something wrong.' Crutch blubbered like he was terrified, which wasn't far from how he felt. 'I am from Uraskova. Don't know Teevilgrad rules. I am sorry. So sorry.' Then he coughed hard. Half a dozen deep, raspy coughs.

Anton grabbed Crutch under the arm as he doubled over coughing. 'Is alright uncle. You see men running?'

'Yes I see komitav officers running everywhere along street.'

'Is good uncle. You see anyone else?'

'Yes. I see four men in black robes. Go that way. He pointed away from the alley and away from the inn the marines were staying at.

Arch warden Gragor blew his whistle and pointed in the direction Crutch had shown Anton.

'They went that way!'

'I have to go, uncle. Are you okay to get home?'

Crutch coughed. 'Am okay. Just bit of a scare. That's all. Hard for old man.'

'Go straight home, uncle.'

'I will,' said Crutch. 'You are good man, Anton. Hope you find men you chase. Must be bad men.'

Anton ran off with the other komitav officers. Crutch waited until they'd all gone and the street was clear, then walked back down the alley to the sewer grate. He looked down and saw Quicksilver squashing himself into Longshot's back. They were all crushed together as tight as they could get, trying to get as far down the short pipe as they could.

'You look cosy down there,' whispered Crutch.

'Get down here,' whispered Quicksilver.

'No need. They're gone.'

'They're gone?'

'I told them I saw four men in black robes running towards the other side of town.'

'Crutch, I could kiss you now,' whispered Sergeant Zander.

'Might want to get out of the sewer first,' whispered Crutch.

'You should take off those black robes,' whispered Crutch as they climbed out of the sewer. 'If we run into someone, I might be able to talk our way out of it, but not while you're wearing those.'

Crutch hobbled down the side streets to the inn while the other marines followed, staying in the shadows. Crutch would signal them that a street was safe, checking for komitav officers and checking windows without making it obvious to make sure no one watched from inside the buildings he passed.

When they got to the inn, they took the entrance through the alley and slipped inside.

'That went well,' said Quicksilver.

'We spent two days catching cockroaches and rats, risked our lives climbing all over the komitav roof, and we've still got no idea where the vault is,' said Longshot.

'I bet they put a guard on the roof now,' said Crutch.

'We'll have to find another way in,' said Sergeant Zander. 'What about Anton? He works there.'

'I don't think he'll give me a guided tour or tell me anything about what's inside. Asking would be weird and risk making him suspicious.'

'We have to find a way,' said Sergeant Zander. 'We don't have forever. I told Cedric if we're not back by the time the quarantine period is over, then he should assume we're dead and sail.'

'Well, that's a happy thought,' said Longshot.

CHAPTER 24
RAT ON A STICK

The next day, Crutch was hobbling to the soup kitchen when he saw a big, juicy rat sitting right in his path with its back to him. He crept up on it slowly and smacked it in the head with his walking cane.

'Nice,' he said as he gutted it right there in the street.

When he got to the soup kitchen, Yelena was cooking. Nikolai slept in a cradle, away from the cooking fire, but just within her reach.

'I have rat,' said Crutch happily. 'Can put in soup.'

Yelena saw Crutch holding the rat, fur on, head on, and heading for the pot.

'No!'

'What is wrong? Is good rat. I cut its guts out.' He went to throw it in the pot.

Yelena shielded the pot with her body. 'No! No rat!'

Crutch shook his head. It seemed the Estovians had strange ideas about eating, just like the Ironborn. 'Okay. I eat myself.'

He put the rat on a stick and held it over the flame in the cooking fire.

'Keep that away from soup pot,' said Yelena.

'Don't worry. You won't get any,' said Crutch. 'Don't appreciate good food.' As he cooked the rat, Pavee wandered in, looking hungry.

'Pavee, look what I got!'

Pavee ran over and smiled when he saw the rat. 'Is nice and big.'

'I know. You want some?'

'Can I?'

'Of course.'

Pavee and Crutch sat in the kitchen, taking turns chewing off bits of the rat. Yelena watched on, horrified, as she cooked the soup for the urchins.

'Is much better cooked,' said Pavee.

'I know,' said Crutch.

'Can I have eye?'

'You can have both eyes.'

'Really.' Pavee laughed and sucked the eyes out of the rat, chewed, and swallowed. 'Is best part of rat.'

'I know.' Said Crutch as Pavee handed the rat back to him. Crutch bit off the tail and started munching at the base. He turned and smiled at Yelena, the end of the rat's tail hanging out of his mouth.

'You are like animals,' said Yelena.

Crutch still couldn't understand what she was upset about. No wonder the people in Teevilgrad were starving if this is how they reacted to good food.

Chapter 25
If You Give There's Always Enough

Sometimes the urchins would climb on Boulder, or, for the urchins who couldn't climb, Boulder would lift them up and put them on his shoulder or bounce them in his arms as they laughed.

After three days of feeding street urchins from their soup kitchen, word got round the neighbourhood, and something astonishing happened.

An old woman, thin and frail, hobbled in and walked up to Crutch. 'I hear you run this soup kitchen?'

'Is soup kitchen of True Compatriots,' said Crutch. 'Would you like soup?'

'I am old woman; live in Teevilgrad my whole life. Never see anyone do anything for street urchins. Is good thing you do. You good people.'

'Thank you. What is your name?'

'I am Leena.'

'Thank you, Leena.'

'I have little but I bring in this bunch of sweet greens I grow on roof of building. I want you to have. For the urchins.'

Crutch was stunned. Here was someone who didn't have enough to eat herself, and she was giving up what little she had to share with others.

'Thank you, Leena. You are good woman.' He took the bunch of greens and gave her a long hug. 'Such a good woman.'

'You keep up good work,' said Leena before she turned and hobbled away, street urchins running around her as she left.

Just a few minutes later, a thin woman in her twenties came in. She gave Crutch half of an old, dried sweet potato. Then it was one person after another. After an hour, they had to line up to bring in food.

'What is going on?' said Crutch.

'Is Teevilgrad way for poor people,' said Yelena. 'We say, 'If you never give, you never have enough. If you give, there's always enough.''

Crutch stood there with his mouth open for a long moment. When he got his composure back, he said, 'Yelena, we can't let these people give us their food then starve. Can True Compatriots tell everyone we have soup if you're hungry?'

'Anton can do this, but thousands of people will come.'

'We'll feed them,' said Crutch. And overnight Anton will have thousands of followers, thought Crutch. He just had to figure out how to feed them all.

Cedric had taught Crutch about logistics since his first days on the Auld Faithful in the animal pens. Then it was making sure you gave the animals just the right amount of food and water so you never ran out. And taking on the right amount when you were in port.

It was part math, part bookkeeping, and part art. Cedric taught him what to do when things went wrong, like when the animal's water went sour, or there wasn't enough food for the pigs. You fed them less, or you killed a pig, or you found other solutions. It was like a giant puzzle you had to remake every day to keep everything running perfectly.

When Cedric beat Wyld in a duel and became captain of the Auld Faithful, he taught Crutch the logistics of running a ship. And on a ship, it was all about feeding the men.

This was the same, but with a lot more people. Yelena said thousands of people would come. Crutch estimated the community dance hall could hold three thousand people standing, so that was a good starting point. On land, he could get food every day, so the logistics weren't that different to feeding a ship's crew for a couple of months. Crutch could run carts to the docks all day long too.

His biggest problem was labour. The young men in the True Compatriots worked during the day. He had the marines, but they had other tasks. Also, it was a risk to expose them too much to Estovians, and four men wasn't enough for the work he needed done, even when you included Boulder, who was worth three men by himself.

As he sat in the dance hall, watching street urchins sliding across the floor playing, the solution hit him in the face. Literally. One of the kind, older street urchins showed a younger urchin how to slide on the wood floor. Distracted, he slid straight into Crutch. Crutch made a show of falling over like an old man.

The street urchin was horrified. 'Are you alright, Crujge? Did I hurt you? So sorry.'

'Am fine,' said Crutch. 'What is your name?'

'I am Dima. So sorry, Crujge.'

'Is really okay. You look strong, Dima,' Crutch lied. He looked scrawny and weak, like nearly everyone else in Teevilgrad.

'I am strong,' said Dima.

'Think you can lift crate or barrel?'

'I do.'

'What about friends? They strong too?'

'Maybe.'

'Tell all your friends we have competition. See who can lift crates and barrels. If you can lift, you win.'

'Is there prize for winners?'

'Of course.'

Dima ran off and got around fifty street urchins together. Crutch led them to the large storage room in the kitchen, where the barrels and crates were kept. One by one, the urchins tested their strength, trying to lift a crate, then a barrel. Nearly half of them could lift both. Simple as that, Crutch had his dock workers.

He told them the prize was to go on a trip on a wagon to the boats every day. The street urchins were thrilled. Some had been hit or run over by wagons. None had ever got to ride in one.

Chapter 26
The Gift Of Kindness

Crutch loaded as many urchins as could fit in the cart. He left Boulder behind with the rest of the urchins to help with unloading. Hopefully they'd be loading and unloading quite a few carts today.

When he got to the docks, Inspector Petrov was there.

'Crujge. These your street urchins?'

'A few of urchins big enough to carry crates and barrels. I need your help.'

'Of course.'

'Tonight we feed three thousand people. Need as much food as we can get.'

'Three thousand. You have party?'

'No. We let anyone hungry eat at soup kitchen.'

'I hear on street you are feeding urchins. Now I have to come down see for myself.'

'Always welcome Petrov. You are reason all these urchins and hundred more urchins eat every night.'

'And now three thousand more people.'

'Yes.'

'Don't know if I can get that much food. Can try.'

'Anything you can do, Petrov. I be so grateful. You are good man to help.'

'Anything for you and urchins, Crujge. We are all brothers.'

'Yes, brothers,' said Crutch.

Inspector Petrov was a force of nature on the docks. He went from ship to ship, threatening higher tariffs, promising lower tariffs, cajoling, lying, whatever it took. Crate after crate, sack after sack, barrel after barrel came off those ships, and the street urchins loaded them onto the wagon.

Crutch made sure the captains and quartermasters of the ships were happy by overpaying them. But some found out what the food was for and refused the extra money. Some gave him spoiling food free of charge.

One quartermaster led him to a cache of crates that was meant for a noble's home. He gave them all to Crutch and refused to take a single rublet.

'I tell them storm at sea spoiled them. Fuck those fat nobles.'

Crutch would drive the wagon back to the soup kitchen, where Boulder, Pavee, and the other street urchins there unloaded it. The community hall had a huge storage area with doors on to the alley and a door through to the kitchen, so it was perfect for this kind of large scale operation.

Crutch quickly realised he needed a wagon driver, so he trained Dima the older street urchin on each trip. He also trained him on how to direct the urchins as they loaded the wagon to make sure they balanced the weight and got the ideal number of crates and barrels on board. Too little, and you had to make too many trips. Too much, and you'd exhaust the horse, or you might break the axle, a wheel, or the frame of the wagon.

Dima picked it up fast. Tomorrow, he would be good to drive the wagon by himself. Crutch would only need to go on the first trip each day to iron out any problems on the docks with Petrov.

Before the last trip of the day, Crutch asked Petrov for something special. Petrov smiled and emerged ten minutes later, lugging two crates.

'Come, my fellow street urchins,' said Petrov. 'Sugar plums!'
'For us?'
'One crate for you, one crate for urchins unloading crates at soup kitchen,' said Crutch.
'Sugar plums won't eat themselves!' said Petrov.

The urchins laughed as they stuffed the sweet, blue plums in their mouths, smearing their faces and staining their clothes with the blue juice. Crutch looked at Petrov's face, a picture of pure delight watching the children feast.

'How much for sugar plums?' said Crutch.

'They're on me,' said Petrov, smiling. 'Worth every cent.'
'Thank you,' said Crutch.
'Thank you,' said Petrov. 'Is wonderful thing you do.'
'Is wonderful thing we do together.'

Petrov put his hand on his heart and looked as if he was about to cry with joy. 'More tomorrow?'

'More tomorrow,' said Crutch.

The street urchins walked behind the full cart on the way back to the soup kitchen. When they got there, all the street urchins helped unload the last cart of the day, then Crutch gave the urchins who'd worked all day at the soup kitchen the second crate of sugar plums. He gave a few to Boulder too. Boulder and the urchins laughed and ate, adding to their little sea of blue faces and clothes.

'I'm a pumpkin,' said Boulder, smiling with blue teeth and blue juice all over his face.

'I am sugar plum,' said Dima. 'Sugar plum is sweeter.'

Crutch did the math in his head. They had enough food for around fifteen hundred people. They'd have to stretch it out if three thousand people came. And now they had to cook the food.

He had Yelena ask all her friends to bring their largest pots. They wouldn't be using them at home anyway. As night fell, the lines started, and the people just kept coming. Crutch noticed that a large number of them were young women, some with babies, some by themselves.

'Are these single women?' said Crutch.

'Most are widows,' said Anton. 'Especially since Papageenar. Solokov pretends like battle there never happened. But we know young men went to Papageenar; know they never came back.'

Crutch had a sick feeling in his stomach thinking about the Estovian troops who came down the Kona Track over and over and were slaughtered by his men. Such a senseless waste of lives that created the suffering he could see right in front of his eyes.

When people reached the front of the line, Yelena or Anton would ask them if they could cook. They had a small army of people cutting vegetables and tending pots the first night.

This was just as well. For some reason, after he shared the rat with Pavee, Yelena wouldn't let him anywhere near the pots while they were cooking. Not even when he came in with a handful of juicy cockroaches. Crutch must have spent too much time alone on the streets or on a ship with all men on the crew. Sometimes he really didn't understand women.

The thing Crutch didn't factor in was people bringing food with them. Leena, the old lady, hobbled in again with more greens, and she brought a friend, another old lady who walked even slower than Leena.

'This is Monika,' said Leena.

'Nice to meet you, Monika,' said Crutch.

'Leena told me what you do here,' said Monika. 'Couldn't believe it. Is bigger than she said.'

'We feed everyone now,' said Crutch. 'Would you like to stay for soup?'

'Yes,' said Monika. Yes, I would. I don't have anything to bring though.'

'You don't need to bring anything. Soup is free.'

'Free for everyone?' said Monika.

'For everyone,' said Crutch. 'Especially you and Leena.'

Monika looked like she was about to burst into tears. She grabbed Crutch in a fierce hug.

'You are wonderful man.'

As the night went on, Leena and Monika set up a little space for babies that was in full view of the kitchen. They'd care for the babies of the mothers who were cooking and any other mothers who needed a break.

When the night was over, Crutch estimated they'd fed at least four thousand people, and there was enough for everyone. *If you give, there's always enough.*

The people walking through the doors were like beaten dogs, dragging their feet, all hope absent from their eyes. But something magical was happening. The women and men recruited to cook in the kitchen started talking with each other. Then they started laughing and joking.

Once people ate, many stayed to help. They'd help serve food, or cook, or clean up. Some asked if they could take soup home to their family, who were too sick or old to walk to the soup kitchen.

'Of course,' said Crutch. 'Just bring pot and fill up.'

Anton talked to everyone. Old people, young, crippled, sick, he showed love to them all. He would hug them and talk to them, ask them about their problems, if there was any way they could help, and treat them like they were the most important people in the world. If they were too weak to stand, he'd give them a chair.

Anton gave them what many needed even more than food. Some human dignity and kindness.

At the end of the night, as the last of the people left and Crutch thought back to what they'd all achieved together, he realised he'd just had one of the greatest days of his life.

Chapter 27
Made Up Nonsense

Crutch and the marines stood at the edge of Teevilgrad's town square, the People's Plaza. In front of them were thousands of Estovian civilians here to listen to Emperor Igor Solokov's address.

Longshot heard about the address listening to people in the inn through the basement door. The inn was buzzing with the news. Solokov had promised to talk about the food shortages in the city.

Crutch hadn't seen this many Estovians so close together since he and the crew of the Auld Faithful were nearly crushed and beaten to death in Zanithburg. The Estovians were so thin and lifeless, it was like Teevilgrad had crushed and beaten them near to death, and they were waiting, helpless, for the last blow to kill them.

At the front of the huge square was a large platform that towered five yards above the ground. Below that and to the left was a lower wooden platform with a brick wall and a door that led onto it. The gallows.

A horn sounded, and the crowd went silent.

'Hail his magnificence, Emperor Igor Solokov.'

The crowd applauded. A muted applause.

Solokov appeared on the speaking platform wearing gold-coloured robes with a large red sash.

'Compatriots of Teevilgrad, I am just like you.'

Crutch thought that was unlikely. For one thing, Solokov had a decidedly large paunch. Everyone in the crowd was painfully thin.

'I work like you since little boy. Come from humble home. I struggle just like you.'

Crutch knew Solokov was born to wealth in a family of nobles and lived a life of privilege.

'I know you are hungry. Food is short. I am hungry too. Filthy Ironworm ships stop food reaching Teevilgrad. They try to starve Estovians. Ironworm are evil scum.'

The crowd started booing. What Solokov was saying didn't make any sense. Most of Teevilgrad's food was grown in Uraskova. Yes, it came by ship, but Estovian warships controlled the ocean between Teevilgrad and Uraskova. Ironborn ships didn't have any way to stop ships on that route. The food wasn't getting to Teevilgrad because it was rotting in the fields after Solokov forced all the young men in Uraskova to join the army or the navy.

'Ironworm scum try to starve you. They want you dead. We must fight them. We must kill them all.' The crowd roared in anger. 'Need every man to join army or navy and fight these scum.' The crowd roared again.

'But there is much bigger problem. Your Komitav discover group of men here in Teevilgrad work in secret to steal food from shops, extort shopkeepers and merchants to put up prices. These evil men make you pay terrible prices.' The crowd was silent as Solokov made this new revelation. Now their anger started boiling.

'I say to Komitav, find these men. They steal food, they put up prices, they must die. I give you, for execution today, the evil conspirators, the Brothers of Mercy.'

The Brothers of Mercy? This was made-up nonsense. Crutch knew the brothers were a military order once, but that was hundreds of years ago. Now they lived lives of voluntary poverty. The one time Crutch met one of the Brothers of Mercy in the streets of Ironbay, the brother gave him the one copper he had. Then he apologised, saying that he had nothing more to give him but words of kindness.

Arch Warden Gragor and five other komitav officers in black uniforms and red sashes pushed six of the brothers in their distinctive blue robes up onto the gallows platform. The Estovians in the crowd were screaming now. Those close enough were spitting at the brothers. Crutch figured they'd probably throw rotten vegetables at them if they had any, but these Estovians would have eaten their rotten vegetables long ago.

One brother tripped on his robe and fell to the ground. The komitav officer kicked him in the guts, then yanked him to his feet by his hair. The crowd roared their approval.

The Estovians started chanting. 'Die, die, die, die!'

'Nothing like a good hanging to get people's minds off their problems,' whispered Sergeant Zander.

Crutch nodded. There were six nooses on the gallows, and conveniently, exactly six Brothers of Mercy 'conspirators'. This barbarity was a method straight out of the book Magnificent Control, Magnificent Victory. Give the population a minority to blame for their troubles to take their focus off the government.

Seeing innocent people about to die just to manipulate the opinion of the people of Teevilgrad was an evil Crutch had never imagined was possible. His guts churned at the thought that his soup kitchen might have caused this.

As the crowd chanted for blood, the komitav officers forced nooses over the six brothers then looked up at Emperor Solokov, who had a sword with a golden handle raised in the air. Solokov dropped his sword and yelled, 'Liberty for all!'

The Komitav pulled the levers, and five brothers fell through the trap doors, their bodies jerking as they reached the ends of their ropes. The Estovians roared their approval.

One brother was left standing on a trap door that didn't spring. Arch Warden Gragor pounded on the trap door with his foot, but it wouldn't open. He pulled out a dagger, held the brother's head with one hand, and cut his throat with the other, blood pouring from the brother's neck as his body flopped on the wooden planks of the gallows.

The Estovians roared and cheered. Crutch and the marines had seen enough. They slipped away, leaving the chanting and cheering of the crowd behind them.

'It's a bad time to be one of the Brothers of Mercy,' whispered Sergeant Zander.

'It's a bad time to be an Estovian,' whispered Crutch.

Chapter 28
I Am Wonderful

More people came to the soup kitchen that night. Emperor Solokov could say whatever he liked about the Brothers of Mercy jacking up food prices, but when people went to the stores or the markets, the food there was just as expensive, and for most of them, the prices were way too high for them to afford enough for a full meal. That was if there was enough food to make a full meal.

The lines had grown from the previous night. More people were bringing pots and taking soup back home with them for their family or neighbours who couldn't come. They fed everyone, and many of the people who came milled around and talked afterwards.

Crutch saw Pavee, Dima, and the street urchins laughing and playing. Now they were eating every day, their sense of adventure and fun had returned. As the night got to its busiest, Inspector Petrov appeared at the entrance. He looked around and saw the street urchins playing.

'My fellow urchins!' he yelled with his arms wide.

They ran to him. Some hugged his legs, and he lifted others up into his arms, smiling like a fighter just handed a trophy for winning a bout.

'We got a new song,' said one small urchin.

'A new song. Well, sing it for me,' said Petrov.

The children looked up at him, smiling, and sang.

'Got too much, but still wants more.

'Ee-or, ee-or, fat pig Igor.'

Then the urchins rolled around on the floor, snorting like pigs and laughing.

'Is catchy,' said Petrov. 'I like. But maybe not sing too much. Might hurt Igor's feelings.'

'Igor is fat pig,' said Dima and snorted.

'This type of talk not nice,' said Petrov. 'You be good urchins. Be nice. Don't talk about Igor. Can you do this for me?'

'Okay Petrov.'

'We love you, Petrov.'

'I love you too, my fellow urchins,' said Petrov, a smile on his face and a tear in his eye.

Petrov saw Crutch. 'Crujge!' He walked straight to Crutch and pulled him into a hug. 'When you tell me how many people you feed, I think you exaggerate. Is much bigger than I thought.'

'Because of your help,' said Crujge. 'Could never get enough food without you.'

'Yes. I know I am wonderful, but you can tell me often as you like. Is good.'

'You're wonderful,' said Crutch.

'Is good. One more time.'

'You're wonderful.'

'Thank you, but stop. Is enough.'

'Will you be okay?' said Crutch. 'Is not safe for you now.'

'Was never safe. Before I do everything for myself. But now,' Petrov looked around at all the people eating, full of life, full of hope. 'Now I am part of this! Is magnificent!'

Later that night, a quiet man came up to Crutch.

'I am Talius.'

'Nice to meet you, Talius. I am Crujge.'

Talius seemed guarded, like he had a heavy burden on his shoulders that he didn't want to carry alone but was too afraid to share.

'Have you heard of Brothers of Mercy?' Talius had leaned in, whispering.

This treaded on dangerous territory, but Crutch followed his instincts and took a chance.

'Since Solokov in People's Plaza, everyone has heard,' said Crutch in a whisper. 'But I travel as merchant many years and know

Brothers of Mercy. They take vow of poverty. Have no use for money. Give every copper they get away to poor.'

'So Brothers of Mercy don't put up food prices?'

'No,' said Crutch. 'Is ridiculous. Brothers of Mercy are good people. No need for money. Have nothing to do with food prices.'

'What about conspiracy?'

'Only conspiracy is Igor getting fat while Teevilgrad starves,' whispered Crutch. Talius looked at Crutch in silence for a long time. If Crutch had judged this wrong, then he was dead. But now he'd gone down this path, there was no turning back.

'So you wouldn't hurt a brother?'

'Never,' said Crutch. 'Would only help. They are victims of lies told to people of Teevilgrad. Is not right.' Crutch coughed and wheezed a little.

'Are you alight?' said Talius.

'Sorry, I am old man. Makes me sad to see good people suffer. Is not right. Brothers of Mercy now pay terrible price for war. Is not right. If I could help, I would.'

Talius stared at Crutch again for a long minute.

'My cousin is a brother.'

It was a whisper, as if Talius was terrified of what the words might do, of where they might lead. But it was a whisper born of desperation, and desperation is the fuel for the fire Crutch was in Teevigrad to fan.

'Careful who you say that to,' said Crutch. 'Is not safe.'

'I know. My cousin is hiding, and I don't know what to do. Komitav are hunting for all broth…' Crutch put up his finger, and Talius paused, then went on in a whisper, 'All of them are hunted. If they find him, they kill him. He is good man. Doesn't deserve this.'

'None of them do,' said Crutch. 'Is not right.'

'You say you have ship. Is huge thing to ask. No, I can't.'

'Ask. Is okay,' said Crutch.

'Can you get him out of Teevilgrad? Somewhere safer like Uraskova?'

Crutch thought about it. The best he could do was get someone back to Ironbay. And the chance of that wasn't good. Right now, his own chances of getting back to Ironbay were slim.

'Is dangerous,' said Crutch. 'But I can try.'

'Thank you. You are good man.'

'I am old man. I die soon anyway. If I die helping good people is okay.' Crutch let out a couple of raspy coughs.

Chapter 29
Stoking The Fires

'The soup kitchen is great,' said Sergeant Zander, 'but we need to stoke the fires of dissent with other parts of the population.'

'If we want civil unrest, we need to target people who can fight,' said Crutch.

'There aren't too many young men in Teevilgrad. They were drafted into the army or the navy.'

'That's who I had in mind,' said Crutch.

'Really?'

'Yes. They're going hungry too, but at least they're fed, so they have money, and you know where they go to spend it.'

'Taverns,' said Sergeant Zander.

'Exactly. We could try talking to some drunk navy crew and soldiers in the tavern. We have the coin to buy them drinks. We'd find out pretty quick if we could get some fires burning there.'

'You gonna do that by yourself?'

'I was thinking you could come with me, Sergeant Zander. Your Estovian accent is quite good now. Testing it out on drunk people is a good way to see how well it'll pass.'

Sergeant Zander smiled. 'This means I'll be forced into doing some drinking.'

'Hey, that's not fair,' said Quicksilver. 'I wanna come along too.'

Crutch shook his head. 'Your Estovian accent is still, how do I put this, like an Ironborn dog took a turd in your mouth and you threw up while yelling forged in steel!'

'Yeah, but they'll be drunk.'
'Not that drunk.'
'Still doesn't seem fair.'
'Can I come?' said Longshot. 'I'll just sit there and drink.'
'No.'
'I'm a pumpkin?' said Boulder with a pleading look on his face.
'I'm sorry, Boulder. You can't come either. But we'll try to bring you all back some bottles of beer.'

It seemed crazy. Most of Teevilgrad suffered from some level of hunger; many were starving, and the taverns still had plenty of beer for people who had the money to buy it. The beer wasn't great, though. Someone had watered down the barrels and it was more water than beer.

Sergeant Zander sipped at his beer with a sour look on his face, like he was sucking a melon.

'First beer in weeks, and it tastes like watered-down rat's piss.'

'I was wondering what the other flavour was,' whispered Crutch.

'You want to kick this off?' whispered Sergeant Zander.

Crutch nodded and hobbled to a table with four young soldiers. 'Brave men. Let me buy you all drink.' The soldiers quickly agreed, offering him a seat.

'Get weight off your feet, old man.'

'Thank you. Very kind. Are you back from Papageenar?'

'No. Just doing training here in Teevilgrad.'

'Is good. My friend's son went to Papageenar. Ten ships of Estovians. Only see ten empty ships come back. Hoping you know him.'

'No. We haven't fought in battle.'

'Shame. Maybe he never come back. Hear many die there. Still, you are brave to join army. Especially since… No I can't say.'

'Since what?'

'You can talk here. Is tavern.'

'They say magnificent Emperor Solokov gives special medal for heroes who die in battle. Wants more brave men like you make ultimate sacrifice. Now, head cut off, or body cut in half is okay. You will be hero with medal mother and father can hang on wall. Is great honour.'

The young soldiers didn't seem too enthusiastic about getting a medal.

'Is important brave men like you fight and die. Magnificent sacrifice to protect magnificent Emperor Solokov and magnificent palace. Emperor must have feasts and play with golden poodles, so we know he is better than us. You die for good cause. Drink to your bravery and magnificent sacrifice.'

The soldiers drank but flashed questioning looks at each other.

'I wish I was still young man. I could charge into glorious battle, have my guts cut out, spill all over ground, and know magnificent Emperor Solokov's magnificent gut was safely filled with cakes and pastries. Would be great honour, and they could put my special medal on grave so everyone know after I die.'

'You would want your guts cut out?' said one of the soldiers.

'Is great honour,' said Crutch. 'But doesn't have to be guts. Dying from head cut in half by axe is good too. Even if you die in agony screaming in jungle, you can know Emperor Solokov is safe at home, happy eating with poodle in lap. You do great service. You brave, brave men. Liberty for all!'

You could barely hear the soldiers, 'Liberty for all,' in response.

'I go now; talk to friend. Hope you all get special medal. You deserve it.' Crutch got up and hobbled over to Sergeant Zander, trying not to smile as he went.

Sergeant Zander talked to a drunk Estovian wearing a navy uniform.

'Go out in blaze of glory,' said Sergeant Zander. 'Burning on deck like men at siege of Ironbay. Is good.'

'Is very good,' said Crutch. 'While flesh is burning, you can think about how your sacrifice keeps magnificent Emporer Solokov safe at home.'

'Safe,' said Sergeant Zander, nodding. 'Is good way to die,' said Sergeant Zander. 'Keeping fat Emperor Solokov safe.'

Sergeant Zander's Estovian accent was okay, but Crutch didn't think they should push their luck.

'Sorry to take friend away,' said Crutch. 'Need to get home.'

'Sorry,' said Sergeant Zander, finishing his drink in one mouthful.

'You brave man in magnificent navy. Hope you die magnificent death for glory of Emperor Solokov. As you burn, can be proud.'

Crutch put his mug down on a tavern table and started hobbling for the door.

'Burn and be proud,' said Sergeant Zander.

They visited two more taverns. This time Crutch stuck with Sergeant Zander and limited him to a little of the talking to reduce the risk. If his accent strayed, Crutch could go into a coughing fit and kick Sergeant Zander in the leg to cover it up. At the last tavern, they bought three bottles of beer for Boulder, Longshot, and Quicksilver and headed back to the inn.

'I think that went well,' whispered Sergeant Zander.

'Solokov is gonna have some new recruits who don't see him the way he'd hope, that's for sure.' Crutch laughed.

'What is it?' whispered Sergeant Zander.

'Burn and be proud,' whispered Crutch. They both burst into laughter.

Chapter 30
The Brothers Of Mercy

Crutch met Talius outside a run-down building not far from the soup kitchen.

'Thank you for meeting me,' said Talius.

'Let's get inside,' whispered Crutch. 'Not safe talking in street.'

'Of course.'

Talius led him down a narrow staircase into a large basement with large rock walls. Crutch hobbled down slowly, with Talius waiting at the bottom.

'Sorry I am slow in my old age,' said Crutch. 'Mind is willing, but body is weak.'

'Is okay,' said Talius.

When Crutch got to the bottom of the stairs, the basement was so dark he couldn't see more than two feet. Talius lit a candle, and to Crutch's surprise, there were three men standing in front of him.

'These are all Brothers of Mercy,' said Talius.

Crutch looked at them all. Thin, hungry, but strangely peaceful.

'Was only expecting one,' said Crutch.

'Sorry I did not explain better.'

'Is okay,' said Crutch.

'This is my cousin Torge. He is good man.'

'If they are Brothers of Mercy, they are all good men,' said Crutch.

'Thank you,' said Torge in a calm, almost monotone voice. 'We brothers strive to do good. This is brother Rohan and brother Martov.'

'How long you hide here?' said Crutch.

'Two weeks ago, member of Anton's group from komitav warn us that Solokov is hunting brothers. We hide then. Some brothers not so lucky to get word early.'

'Is wrong,' said Crutch, then coughed deep and raspy.

'Sounds like bad cough,' said Torge.

'Is okay. I am old. Something has to kill me.'

'Talius says you might help us?'

'I can try,' said Crutch.

Crutch didn't know why he was going out on a limb to help the brothers. He couldn't see a way to use it to the advantage of the marines' mission. But some things you do because they help you, and some things you do just because they're the right thing to do.

If he let the brothers get murdered by Solokov when he could have helped them, he knew that would grind on his mind for years to come.

'Do you brothers have skills?'

'Of course. Can grow food, brew beer, cook, sew, clean.'

'Is good,' said Crutch, hiding his disappointment.

'Also fight,' said Torge.

'Fight?' said Crutch.

'Is tradition. Brothers of Mercy were warriors two hundred years ago before swearing to life of peace, poverty, and chastity. We still train every day. Is ritual.'

'It is?'

'Yes.'

'I'd love to see. You have weapons?'

'No need. Mind is weapon. Brothers of Mercy can use anything.'

'Can you demonstrate?'

'Of course.' Torge motioned to Rohan. They faced off with each other.

Torge and Rohan spun around, keeping out of punching range, one jumping forward, then the other. Then Torge slammed his foot into Rohan's knee, driving him to the ground, and leapt down on him with an elbow to the face. Torge stopped his elbow strike an inch from Rohan's eye.

Then he put out his hand and pulled Rohan up to his feet. 'Had to strike fast this time,' said Torge. 'Since last time you beat me with broomstick. Hit you before you have chance.'

'Is good idea,' said Rohan, rubbing his knee. 'I must find way to beat fast strike now.'

'Wise.'

Crutch hid his excitement, but inside he was delighted. These brothers were stone cold killers, and he could use as many stone cold killers as he could get!

'Is good,' said Crutch. 'Will you fight komitav to save brothers?'

'We talk about this,' said Torge. 'Brothers of Mercy have not fought in two hundred years.'

'But no one has tried to kill us in two hundred years,' said Rohan.

'We must fight,' said Martov. 'We train to protect innocent and protect brotherhood.'

'Martov is youngest brother. Is not so simple,' said Torge.

Martov nodded respectfully to Torge.

'The komitav will kill you all in public execution to keep war with Ironbay alive,' said Crutch. 'You are now piece on Solokov's game board.'

'Talius said you might get us out of Teevilgrad?' said Torge. 'Away from komitav?'

'I can try,' said Crutch. 'But chance is, some time in escape, you fight komitav or die.'

Torge nodded. Then he dropped his head in deep thought. After a few seconds, he raised his head and said, 'Then we fight.'

Chapter 31
No I Am Pumpkin

'We have a serious problem,' said Sergeant Zander when Crutch got back from meeting the Brothers of Mercy. 'While you were gone, Boulder was taken by the komitav.'

'What?'

'Your street urchin Pavee told me Boulder was out in the alley at the soup kitchen lifting food crates when half a dozen komitav arrested him.'

A huge shot of fear went up Crutch's spine. 'Did he fight?' If he did, their chances of getting him out were near zero. They'd know he was a soldier of some kind.

'Pavee said he went quiet as a kitten.'

Crutch realised he'd been holding his breath and took a deep breath in. *Good work, Boulder.* 'Do we know where he is?'

'Those street urchins really love you and Boulder. They followed him all the way to Komitav Operative. They took him in the main entrance. Pavee said the urchins tried to go in, but the komitav threatened to kill them if they did.'

'I'm going there now, said Crutch.

Crutch took as many back alleys as he could so he could go full speed in the shadows of the walls, driving along on his walking cane and his good leg. He'd slow to his painfully slow hobble when he had to go on a main street or anyone was around.

He got to the main building and hobbled up to the komitav officers guarding the entrance.

'Good day, compatriot,' said Crutch. 'Your officers brought in worker of mine. Very big man, thinks he is pumpkin. I think they do me favour.'

The guards tried to keep a straight face but couldn't.

'We saw human pumpkin,' said the first guard.

'Huge human pumpkin,' said the second, and they both laughed.

'That's him.' Crutch spun his finger around his ear to make the crazy sign and smiled. 'He is harmless but sometimes gets lost. I think maybe my nephew Anton Ivenko brought him.'

'Your nephew is Anton Ivenko?'

'Yes.'

'Anton is good man. Brings us food.'

'Yes, he is very good man. I am very proud uncle.' Crutch made a couple of deep, raspy coughs.

'Are you okay?' said the first guard.

'Just old. The walk over here maybe too much for old man.'

'Come on, old man. I'll walk you in.' The guard held him under the arm of his bad leg.

'Thank you. You are kind. You know my nephew Anton.'

'Only a little. He brings food to guards when he can.'

'He is such good boy,' said Crutch.

As they hobbled along the maze of corridors and rooms, Crutch tried to memorise them all. Some doors were closed, some open. Through the open doors, Crutch could see komitav officers with their black uniforms and their red sashes. Even the komitav officers looked starved.

After five minutes of hobbling, the guard stopped outside a closed door.

'Wait here for second. I will get Anton.'

Crutch stood there in the corridor outside the door, trying to remember everything he saw. He wondered what was going on behind that door. Were they torturing Boulder? Had he already given up the information that would get them killed? Was he already dead? Just the thought of Boulder tortured or killed filled Crutch with an unbearable grief.

Anton came running up the corridor, breaking Crutch's thoughts.

'They told me they arrested Boulder,' said Anton.

'Yes,' said Crutch. 'Guard brought me to this door.'

'Is not right,' said Anton. He pounded on the door.

A voice came from the other side. 'We are interrogating suspect. Don't want to be disturbed.'

'This is officer Anton Ivenko. Open door now!'

Crutch could hear the unlatching of the door, and a komitav officer peered out.

'Anton. What is problem?'

'You have my uncle's worker in there.'

'Your uncle?'

'Let us in,' said Anton. He pushed at the door, shoving the komitav officer out of the way. Another officer stood over Boulder, who sat in a chair. Or the komitav officer would have stood over him if Boulder wasn't so tall. Even sitting, Boulder's head was at the same level as the komitav officer.

Boulder looked up, saw Crutch hobbling in, smiled, and said, 'I'm a pumpkin.'

'Why did you arrest this man?' said Anton.

'Orders,' said the first komitav officer. 'Written orders said he might be threat.'

'Is not a threat,' said Anton. 'The man thinks he is vegetable.'

'Is true. We have him here for two hours, and all he says is, 'I am pumpkin, I am pumpkin. Problem is, he says it in Ironborn accent.'

'His grandma from Ironbay raised him,' said Crutch. 'He is simple man, like boy. Doesn't say much, but that's where accent comes from.'

'He is your worker?' said the first komitav officer.

'Yes. He is good for lifting large crates and barrels. I am old man. Can't do this any more. All young men gone to army. Army don't want him so I hire.' Crutch coughed half a dozen times, wheezing at the end.

'I'm a pumpkin,' said Boulder.

'Sorry my compatriots bring in your worker,' said Anton. 'Can he take his human vegetable back home now?'

The komitav officers laughed. 'Okay. Sorry Crujge. Anton is good man. You can go. Take pumpkin with you.'

'Thank you, compatriots,' said Anton, helping guide Crutch away.

'Thank you, compatriots,' said Crutch. 'Come on, Boulder.'

As they walked away, they could hear the Komitav officers laughing.

'I am pumpkin.'

'No. I am pumpkin.'

'Don't take personally,' said Anton. 'They are good men. Have to follow orders.'

'Is okay,' said Crutch. 'Thank you for your help. You are good nephew.'

'Of course. Boulder is good man. Street urchins love him at soup kitchen.'

'Good man,' said Crutch. 'Good friend.'

'I'm a pumpkin,' said Boulder, grinning.

Crutch and Anton laughed, and Boulder laughed with them.

'I take you out through shortcut,' said Anton. 'Save your legs.'

'Thank you, Anton. You are very kind.'

Crutch memorised the path they took. He was glad now that he limped like an old man. The layout of the corridors disoriented him and made little sense. They were obviously arranged that way to make it as difficult as possible for anyone breaking into the building to find a room they were looking for. And to make it as difficult as possible for a prisoner to escape.

When he saw it, he stopped in surprise, then covered up by coughing hard and wheezing.

'You okay, uncle?'

'Just need second to catch breath.' Crutch looked down the corridor on his right, out of the side of his eye. He could only just see it in a room off the corridor, but it was there. The vault. Two komitav guards in front of it.

The glowstone would be there behind that massive steel door. He was so close, but he might as well be in Ironbay. There was no way he could get into that vault with komitav officers and guards everywhere. But now he knew exactly where the vault was.

'I am okay now. Thank you, Anton. You are kind to wait for me.'

'You sure you're okay?'

'Yes,' said Crutch, taking a last glance at the vault. 'Have my strength back now.'

As they made their way through the corridors, Crutch's mind was spinning and grinding, making a mental note of everything he saw. They came to a door with two komitav guards who immediately recognised Anton, nodded, and opened the door for him.

Then they were outside in an alley. A quiet alley off the main street. Crutch could hug someone now, and Anton was closest so he did.

'Thank you, Anton. After you, Boulder is closest I have to family,' said Crutch, his words filled with gratitude. Gratitude for helping him find the glowstone.

'Is okay uncle. You need help getting home?'

'No. Boulder can help.' Boulder took Crutch's arm, smiling.

'I'm a pumpkin,' said Boulder.

'Okay. Be careful,' said Anton.

Crutch hobbled down the alley towards the main street, with Boulder making a good show of helping him. It was all he could do not to run to the inn and tell Sergeant Zander and the other marines he'd found the glowstone.

'Good work, Boulder,' whispered Crutch. You gave the komitav nothing to work with.'

Boulder grinned next to him.

'I knew you'd get me out,' whispered Boulder. 'You're my friend.'

'So we know exactly where the vault is now,' said Sergeant Zander, excited when Crutch and Boulder got back to the inn and Crutch shared the good news with them.

'But how do we get in to the Komitav Operative building?' said Longshot. 'We couldn't even walk over the roof without setting off the guards.'

'Getting in is just part of the problem,' said Crutch. The vault door is massive. We'll need a key to open it.'

'Let's do what we can do first,' said Sergeant Zander. 'If we're gonna get into the Komitav Operative building, we need the komitav busy elsewhere. Time to sow as much discontent as we can.'

'You and Crutch are going drinking again, aren't you Sarge?' said Quicksilver.

'We are,' said Sergeant Zander.

'And you're leaving us behind?' said Longshot.

'We are,' said Sergeant Zander. 'But there is something I want you and Quicksilver to take a look at for me.'

Chapter 32
Some Things You Cant Fake

Crutch and Sergeant Zander were in a tavern they hadn't visited before 'encouraging' the new army and navy recruits to bathe themselves in glory in battles hundreds of miles away to ensure Emperor Solokov could maintain his sumptuous lifestyle in the Teevilgrad palace.

The navy recruit at their table had run outside to vomit up his cheap, watered-down beer and his pork dinner after Crutch described how glorious it would be to be shot through the groin by a giant bolt from a ballista and get pinned to the mast while the ship was on fire.

'Your flesh will burn like magnificent torch to light way for Emperor Solokov's swim in palace pool with golden poodle. Smell will be like pork burning. Even after you dead from face melting, name will live forever on tiny gravestone in Teevilgrad.'

The recruit ran past a slim, attractive woman in a tight red dress that had a slit up the side all the way to the waist. Crutch noticed when they came in that this tavern had a musician playing in the corner and several whores milling around, offering to take a navy man or a soldier upstairs for a piece of silver.

The woman in the red dress came to their table, sat down on the bench Crutch was on, and slid right up next to him. She slid a mug across to Sergeant Zander, smiled, and said, 'That's for you.'

Sergeant Zander sniffed at the drink in the mug. 'Honeysap rum.'

'Premium,' said the woman.

Sergeant Zander took a careful sip, and his face lit up with a smile. 'Is premium. Thank you.'

The woman ran her finger over Crutch's chest. It slowly slid down till it got to Crutch's waist.

'I am old man,' said Crutch. 'Equipment down there only good for pissing. Even that not good.'

'Orange rock,' said the woman.

'What you say?' said Crutch.

'Orange rock.'

Crutch looked at her. Her face was inches from his. 'Did Jasper send you?' he whispered.

'I am Jasper.'

She turned the hand that was on his waist over so he could see her palm. She rubbed away some face paint to reveal a faded heart in intricate detail, with the name Rosee written below it. Crutch was stunned. How could this be Jasper?

'Don't talk here,' whispered Jasper. 'I have a room upstairs. Both of you come with me.'

Jasper grabbed Crutch's shirt and pulled him along behind her while he hobbled as quick as he could to keep up. Crutch signalled for Sergeant Zander to follow. He sculled his mug of honeysap rum, then fell in behind them, a confused look on his face.

Jasper strutted, every step a display of sexiness, her heels clicking on the wood of the tavern floor, then the tavern steps, as they made their way up the stairs. Jasper led them through a solid wood door and closed it behind them.

'Maybe I leave alone,' said Sergeant Zander. 'Don't want to watch.'

'We can talk softly here,' said Jasper. 'The walls and the door are thick, and the music is loud.'

'This is Jasper,' said Crutch.

'No,' said Sergeant Zander. 'Jasper is a man.'

'Apparently not,' said Crutch. 'She showed me her identification. Something you can't fake. This is Jasper.'

'Hello, Sergeant Zander. I did promise you a mug of honeysap rum.' Sergeant Zander stood with his mouth open. 'Premium as promised.'

'By the gods,' said Sergeant Zander.

'Good to see you're still alive,' said Jasper. 'You've been busy. Do I need to ask whose idea the soup kitchen was?'

There was a pause as Sergeant Zander tried to process what was happening. 'That was Crutch,' he said, still staring dumbfounded at Jasper.

'Of course it was. In espionage, there are great ideas, then there is art. The soup kitchen is a masterpiece. Truly inspired. Our sources say Solokov is beside himself with anger.'

'The Brothers of Mercy paid a heavy price for that,' said Crutch.

'Solokov is flailing around, trying to get back the control over his people he's losing,' said Jasper. 'The Brothers of Mercy won't be the last of his victims. Expect something much bigger, much worse.'

'That's something to look forward to,' said Sergeant Zander. He still looked at Jasper as if his eyes had somehow failed him.

'Why are you in Teevilgrad?' said Crutch.

'I came to help,' said Jasper. 'No one in the Ironbay navy office thought you'd get this far. No one except me. I insisted you would need help, and after two weeks of browbeating anyone who would listen to me and quite a few who wouldn't, they finally told me if I was so determined to get you help, I should do it myself. So here I am.'

'Here you are,' said Sergeant Zander, still in some form of shock.

'There is something we need,' said Crutch. 'We know exactly where the glowstone is.'

'Nice work, marines.'

'There's a vault in the Komitav Operative building. We need a key to that vault to get the glowstone out.'

Jasper nodded. 'It won't be easy to get. We may have to work on getting it together.'

'Of course,' said Crutch.

'I'll be in touch,' said Jasper, walking over to Sergeant Zander. 'Better not stay here too long. It might bring some heat.' She pushed her body up against Sergeant Zander's side.

'Okay,' said Crutch.

'I've never told you this before, Sergeant Zander, but you're really quite handsome.' She ran a finger across his cheek to his lips.

'Thank you, Jasper,' Sergeant Zander stuttered.

'Oh please. We'll be working close together now.' Jasper ground her hips against Sergeant Zander's. 'So close, it's almost like we're lovers. Call me Jas.'

'Okay.'

'Time to go,' said Crutch.

'Yes, time to go,' said Jasper. 'Unless you'd like to stay here for a while, Sergeant Zander. With me.'

'Um. I'd better stick with Crutch,' said Sergeant Zander.

'Okay,' said Jasper, her face still inches from Sergeant Zander's. 'See you soon.'

Sergeant Zander extracted himself from Jasper and almost fell over backwards pulling away. Crutch and Sergeant Zander made their way down the stairs, Crutch hobbling slowly down with his cane. Once they were outside, they headed straight for the inn.

'Jasper is a woman,' said Sergeant Zander. The marines huddled together in the basement of the inn.

'A woman?' said Longshot. 'No. Jasper is a man.'

'She's a woman,' said Sergeant Zander.

'So a short, fat woman?'

'No,' said Sergeant Zander. 'A stunning, gorgeous, slim woman with breasts and legs and painted lips.'

'How much did you drink?' said Longshot. 'Did you get on the honeysap rum again?'

'No. I mean, yes, I had some honeysap rum, but Jasper is a woman.'

'Could you clear this up for us, Crutch? Sergeant Zander is telling us Jasper is a woman.'

'It's true,' said Crutch. 'My best guess is she disguised herself as a man in Ironbay. Jasper is definitely a woman. Or brilliantly disguised as a woman.'

'She's a woman,' said Sergeant Zander.

'You would know,' said Crutch. 'You pressed right up against her with your hips grinding together.'

'It's okay, Sarge,' said Longshot. 'We've seen a lot of this in the navy. We don't judge you.'

'Love is love,' said Boulder.

'She's a woman!' said Sergeant Zander.

'Keep your voice down,' whispered Crutch.

'Are you sure it's Jasper?' said Quicksilver. 'Could be someone pretending to be Jasper.'

'It's Jasper,' said Crutch. 'She showed me something that you can't fake to prove it was her.'

'Not her…' Quicksilver pointed to his crotch.

'No, not that,' said Crutch.

'She came here to help us,' said Sergeant Zander. 'She's gonna help us get the key to the vault.'

'And she's a woman?'

'Yes.'

'I'm a pumpkin,' said Boulder.

'From what I've seen tonight,' said Sergeant Zander, 'that seems quite possible.'

'Love is love?' said Crutch.

'Grandma taught me that,' said Boulder.

Chapter 33
Food Seizures

Inspector Petrov met Crutch at the docks with the wagon to start the daily food pick-up, but they had a problem.

'His magnificence, Emperor Solokov, is seizing food from ships,' said Petrov. 'Is not even paying for it.'

'Is not right,' said Crutch. 'So no food today?'

'What you think?' said Petrov, smiling.

Crutch laughed. 'I think you come up with plan.'

'You know me too well,' said Petrov. 'After I see food seizure in first ship, I tell captains and quartermasters of other ships to hide some food. Tell them you will come and pay them well for it; stop them losing money. Every ship has places to hide cargo. I know this. I am inspector for border patrol.'

'Inspector Petrov, you are genius.'

'I know,' said Petrov, smiling.

Crutch thought about how he'd get the food into the city to the soup kitchen. He didn't want to make it too obvious they were carrying wagons full of food, just in case Solokov's loyal men seized the wagon.

He got the street urchins to put the crates and barrels on the bottom of the wagon, covered them with a blanket, and put a layer of empty crates and barrels on top. Then they drove through the city, looking as miserable as possible.

Crutch took a different route each time he went through the city up and back to the docks, taking side streets so the same people wouldn't see them going to the docks with a wagon over and over. It wasn't perfect. The sailors on the docks could see them loading food, but Petrov told him, after the seizures, Crutch was the only person paying them any money.

Before Crutch turned up, the sailors worried they wouldn't be paid. Petrov had told them not to talk about where they got their money from, and the captains and quartermasters were already silent. They didn't want to face execution for hiding the food.

Crutch knew he'd need a better system if Solokov continued the food seizures.

During that day, when Crutch was at the soup kitchen unloading, a couple of men in their fifties came down the alley with a horse and wagon.

One of the men walked up to Crutch. 'You'd be Crujge?'

'I am.'

'I am Barlovi. Me and Ritnen spent last few nights sneaking down Kodil Bay.'

'Kodil Bay?' said Crutch. 'I hear is full of crocs.'

'One less croc,' said Barlovi. 'We caught one last night.'

'How you get back through gates? Is forbidden to go into quarantine zone.'

'Just told them croc is for True Compariots soup kitchen. Watchmen there said, 'My ma goes to soup kitchen. Other guard says, 'I go to soup kitchen myself.' We all laugh; they let us straight through.'

Crutch hobbled down to the wagon. Some blankets covered the croc. It was so large, they'd bent its tail to get it into the wagon and still its head hung out the back.

Crutch was thrilled. They could add croc meat to the soup for a week.

'Is huge. Thank you. You both true compatriots. Good men.'

'We go back tonight. See if we catch more.'

'Be careful,' said Crutch. 'Croc make good meal, but maybe croc make meal of you.'

Barlovi and his friend laughed. 'Is true.'

'Boulder and urchins will get croc off wagon. Have some soup before you leave.'

Barlovi looked Crutch in the eyes, shook his hand, and said, 'Thank you Crujge. Because of you, our people eat again, laugh again.'

'Because of all of us together,' said Crutch. 'Includes you now with huge croc. You feed kitchen for whole week.'

Barlovi's face filled with pride, and he pulled Crutch into a hug.

Yelena was thrilled to get the croc meat when she and Anton arrived early in the evening to start the cooking and set up. When he was alone with Yelena Crutch said, 'Could have meat all the time.'

'How?' said Yelena.

'Rat and cockroaches,' said Crutch.

'We not use rat in soup. Or cockroach.'

'Is good.'

'No.'

'But we can get plenty cockroaches,' said Crutch. 'Is good meat.'

'No!'

'Why not?'

'If we put cockroach in soup, no one will eat it.'

'Is okay. We cook and mash up cockroach. No one will know is there. Except for head and legs.'

'Head and legs?'

'Is best part. Crunchy!'

'No!'

Crutch couldn't understand why Yelena was so fixed against putting some cockroaches and rats in the soup. He really didn't understand women. Sergeant Zander had told him some women got moody once a month. He thought maybe it was that.

'I will get cockroach and make soup myself. You will see.'

'No! Anton!'

Anton came running. 'What's wrong, Yelena?'

'Crujge wants to put rat and cockroach in soup.'

Anton looked at Crutch. 'What is this, Crujge?'

'Cockroach is good and plenty nearby.'

Anton looked at Crutch with his mouth open. 'Plenty?'

'Get thousands from the sewers. Street urchins can catch every day to put in soup.'

'From sewers?'

'Yes. Good meat. Not as good as croc or rat, but still good.'

Anton looked at Crutch for a few seconds and started to laugh.

'Why you laugh?' said Yelena. 'Is not funny.'

'I didn't know you were such great jokester, Crujge,' said Anton.

'Is not joke. He ate rat with Pavee here in kitchen.'

'Really?'

'Yes,' said Yelena. 'Pavee sucked eyeballs out of rat, and Crujge chewed on tail with end still hanging out of mouth.'

Anton looked at Crujge for a few seconds and started laughing again.

'Why you laugh?' said Yelena.

'Is fake rat. Before war, I see someone do this. Make fake rat, put fruit in eyes, fake tail from banana rolled up.'

'Fake?' said Yelena.

'Yes, fake,' said Anton. 'Is great joke, Crujge.' He started laughing again, then he couldn't stop. Yelena laughed with him, first softly, then she shrieked with laughter.

'Put cockroach in soup,' said Yelena, doubling over.

'Get from sewers,' said Anton, tears running down his face.

'Crujge told me, told me, head and legs of cockroach best part. Crunchy!' They laughed so hard, Yelena and Anton struggled to stay on their feet. Crutch laughed with them. It was so good to see them happy.

When they finally regained their composure, Anton said, 'Thank you, Crujge. Haven't heard joke like this for years. Haven't laughed like this for years. He walked out of the kitchen into the dance hall, saying, 'Street urchins can get cockroaches from sewers,' and burst into laughter again.

Yelena looked at Crutch smiling and said, 'Crunchy,' then burst into laughter too.

'Have good news for you,' said Crutch when he saw Pavee finishing his meal at the soup kitchen.

'What is that?' said Pavee.

'Rats and cockroaches we catch, we can eat ourselves.'

'No,' said Pavee. 'We should share. Put in soup.'

'They don't want rat or cockroach in soup,' said Crutch. 'Not even head or legs of cockroaches.'

'No,' said Pavee. 'Head and legs best part. Crunchy.'

'I know. But they don't want.'

'Is crazy.'

'That's what I told them,' said Crutch. 'Also, I have mission for you.'

Pavee smiled. It was wonderful to see him smile. Crutch thought about the beat down, emaciated street urchin he was and the change he'd made in just a few weeks.

'Is fun mission?'

'Yes. Do you know run-down building on Sunset Street?'

'I know,' said Pavee.

'Could you take soup to basement there once a day without anyone seeing?'

'Yes, I can do.'

'And don't tell anyone. Not a word. Not even the urchins. Don't let them see either.'

'I can do,' said Pavee.

'You can talk to Torge when you get there.'

'Torge?'

'Yes. Don't tell name to anyone. Don't tell anyone anything.'

'I will do.'

'Thank you Pavee.'

Chapter 34
We Must Dance

That night, Solokov's food seizures had no impact on their ability to serve soup to the people who came. Crutch had already started stockpiling foods that kept longer, just like Cedric had taught him to on the Auld Faithful.

On a ship, you couldn't predict how long it might take to reach the next port, so stocks of food that kept longer were essential. In the storage room next to the soup kitchen, Crutch had sacks of beans, flour, sugar, and piles of yams, all with a huge shelf life. The stockpile also meant they could cook more food if more people showed up.

And there were more food donations, too. People coming to the soup kitchen wanted to give more, and more people were coming.

Leena had taught others how to grow greens on their roofs, and now the soup was full of them. There were other clever ideas. One woman grew yams in pots and ran the vines up the vertical beams of her building. Once she told the True Compatriots what she was doing, yams in pots sprung up at the bottom of every vertical support beam in the neighbourhood. It would take six months to harvest those, but they represented a promise for the future every time he saw them.

If it was Solokov's plan to starve the food kitchen of supplies, he'd failed miserably.

Someone had painted above the entrance doors True Compatriots. Underneath it, *If you give, there's always enough.*'

'For first time since war started, people have hope,' said Anton.

After they started serving soup, an old man carrying a stringed instrument came up to Crutch.

'Good evening,' he said. 'I am Andreas Crossovee, the finest minstrel in all of Teevilgrad.'

'Welcome, Andreas,' said Crutch.

'I must tell you, I injure my elbow last year. Can only play for ten, twenty minutes, then need to rest for night.'

'Am sorry to hear that.'

'But if you give me soup, I will play best twenty minutes of music you ever hear.' Andreas smiled after he said that. Crutch could see there was not a single tooth in his head.

'The soup is free for everyone, Andreas.'

'Is free?'

'For anyone hungry,' said Crutch.

Andreas looked around at the hundreds of people already eating. 'No one pays?'

'No. Is free.'

Andreas threw his arms around Crutch. 'You are wonderful, wonderful man.'

'Thank you,' said Crutch. 'You eat now. Maybe later, after people eat, you play us all tune.'

'I play best music ever.' Andreas looked at all the people working in the kitchen. 'Best music ever for all you wonderful, wonderful people.'

The workers in the kitchen looked up and smiled.

That night was their biggest ever. People started bringing their own chairs so they could sit and talk. There were so many people, the chairs spilled into the street outside, with people talking and laughing.

Petrov arrived with two crates full of honey apples. The children flocked to him. Petrov grinned and laughed as he handed an apple to each child.

'One for you. One for you. Yes, you can have one.'

There were so many children, his crates were empty before he could give them all a honey apple.

'Are you fellow urchins true compatriots?' said Petrov.

'Yes,' said the children in unison.

'Motto of true compatriots is, if you give, there's always enough. Urchins with honey apples, can you be true compatriots and share with urchins who don't have honey apple?'

The children nodded. They laughed as they passed around their half-chewed apples to each other, not caring where they went or where they got the next apple from.

Petrov smiled proudly as he watched them.

Crutch estimated, based on the quantity of food they'd used up, that between people eating in the soup kitchen and people taking soup home, they must have served ten thousand people during the night.

After everyone had eaten, Andreas started picking at his stringed instrument, beginning slowly and rhythmically. People clapped in time, gently at first, then with more vigour.

Petrov strutted in time with the music, walked to the middle of the hall and yelled, 'We must dance!' He stepped from side to side in time, with his arms held out beside his body. Others joined him, so they were arm to arm until they formed a huge circle of men and women stepping in time.

Every few seconds, everyone would yell 'Hey!' in time with the music, and the circle would change and move in the opposite direction.

People from outside crowded round the doors and windows, clapping and yelling in time.

Andreas slowly picked up the pace, with the circle of men and women moving round and round faster and faster, with the clapping getting louder and louder.

In the circle, he saw Yelena and Anton arm in arm, smiling, their eyes never leaving each other as the circle spun around. The speed and intensity of the music, the clapping, and the yells in time grew, until many dancers were barely keeping up. Anton and Yelena laughed with joy, keeping up with the ease of skilled dancers, eyes still locked on each other until the music finally stopped.

The dancers laughed and hugged, while everyone else in the room clapped and cheered. Anton pulled Yelena into his arms, and they kissed. The other dancers parted, and the crowd watched the two young lovers in their own world. They clapped and cheered even louder.

Their lips parted. Anton looked out and saw that the entire room, and people leaning in through the windows and doors, were looking at them, applauding. He whispered something to Yelena. She smiled, then they both stepped so they were holding hands with their arms outstretched between them and took a deep, long bow together. The clapping and cheers grew even louder.

Deep inside, in a part of his mind, Crutch hoped that maybe this would work out. The true compatriots would grow so large that Anton would take over Teevilgrad without a drop of blood being shed. The Estovians would give up the war, and there'd never be another Kona Track, never be another tiny gravestone added to the Rosewood Cemetery, and he'd never have to kill another Estovian who Solokov's thugs had press-ganged into their army.

Then Crutch reminded himself that Igor Solokov would never leave Teevilgrad quietly. He'd torture and execute his way through anyone who threatened his control of the city. And by helping the true compatriots he made them a target just as surely as if he painted a big red mark on their backs. Crutch was swimming in a sea of lies, and the only hope he could afford was that the next lie wouldn't drown them all in a giant wave of blood.

Chapter 35
Feeding The Komitav

That night, after most of the people had left, Crutch talked to Anton. Anton was the happiest Crutch had ever seen him.

'Is amazing,' said Anton. 'First time since war, people danced. We danced!'

'Was beautiful,' said Crutch. 'I am so happy to see. You and Yelena were like fairy tale together.'

'Is all thanks to you, uncle. You make this possible.'

'I just give a little money. You and Yelena and street urchins and everyone else do work.'

'You give more than money,' said Anton. 'You help true compatriot's dream come alive.'

'I have question for you, Anton.'

'Yes.'

'Sometimes you work nights at Komitav?' said Crutch.

'Yes. Is hard to be away from Yelena.'

'Other Komitav officers work at night too?'

'Yes. Many.'

'So they have no way to come to soup kitchen. Go hungry?'

'Yes. Only high-ranked officers get paid enough to eat well.'

'I want to feed them after soup kitchen closes.'

'Crujge, you are amazing man. Always think of more people to help.'

'Just don't like to see people hungry. You can help with this?'

'Of course.'

After the soup kitchen closed, Crutch took Dima and a wagon full of empty barrels to the Komitav Operative building and parked in the alley he'd come out of on the day he retrieved Boulder. Crutch turned the wagon around in the alley and got the back of it nice and close to the door.

Then he knocked on the door. A komitav officer opened it and poked his head out.

'I am Crujge here with food from soup kitchen.'

The komitav officer smiled. 'Crujge, Anton told us you would come.'

They had two large pots of soup in the back of the wagon, each sitting in a crate packed with hay to keep them warm. The komitav officers started coming out of the door with bowls. Crutch and Dima filled up the bowls and chatted to the officers.

'Is good thing you do,' said one.

'Anton says you are great man,' said another.

'No one should go hungry,' said Crutch. 'We are all true compatriots. Must stick together.'

Another officer looked at the wagon as he ate his soup. 'Why so many barrels?'

'We put empty barrels on wagon when we finish unloading at end of day. Take them back to docks in morning for ships to reuse.'

The Komitav officer nodded. 'Thank you for soup. Most nights, we go hungry. Is hard to work.'

'Makes me happy to give you food, compatriot. Work you do keep Teevilgrad and Estovia safe. Should not go hungry.'

'Is good,' said the Komitav officer. 'Anton said you are good man. Now I see why.'

'I am just humble merchant try to make little difference to people of Teevilgrad. You Komitav are great men. Always feel safe when I see black uniform and red sash.'

After the first night, Crutch let Dima and his best friend, another urchin Tamiva, take the wagon to the Komitav Operative building. He figured they were safe enough. The Komitav officers appreciated being fed.

Crutch told Dima to make sure and park the wagon close to the door every night with the rear of the wagon right near the door to make it faster and easier to serve the soup.

Chapter 36
Igor's Kitchen

Crutch and the marines stood watching the People's Plaza. Emperor Solokov had announced food at the plaza, whatever that meant. The marines figured it would be a good idea to find out.

The People's Plaza was packed, with even more people than for the executions of the Brothers of Mercy. On the gallows platform were Arch Warden Gragor and his five men, all wearing their black uniforms with red sashes.

'Looks like another execution,' whispered Crutch.

'Best way to cheer up the local population,' whispered Sergeant Zander.

As they stood there, the crowd grew even larger. They crushed into the plaza so tight, they couldn't move. Crutch and marines were on the other side of the road away from the plaza. From where they stood in the shadows, they had a good view of the gallows and the high platform they expected Emperor Solokov to come out on.

He didn't disappoint. A horn sounded, and a herald announced, 'Hail his magnificence, Emperor Igor Solokov.'

Solokov strutted to the front of his platform in his golden robes with a red sash.

'Is he thinner?' whispered Sergeant Zander.

It was hard to tell from this distance, but Solokov did look thinner.

'Has he bandaged up his gut or something so he'll look skinny?' whispered Crutch.

'Wouldn't surprise me,' whispered Sergeant Zander. 'Wants to look like he's one of the people. Hard to do that when they're all starving and you're a fat toad.'

'People of Teevilgrad,' said Solokov. 'I am one of you. I go hungry just like you.'

'Perfect guess Crutch,' whispered Sergeant Zander.

'He's the perfect arsehole,' whispered Crutch.

'I scour ships and seize food being sent to Brothers of Mercy so you can eat.'

'He what?'

'Today is food at plaza. Down here, Arch Warden Gragor and his magnificent komitav wardens give you food. All free.'

One of Gragor's wardens pulled a blanket away and revealed around twenty crates of food. So this was Solokov's answer to the threat the soup kitchen posed to his control of Teevilgrad. A half-arsed attempt to give away food. He wasn't even cooking it into soup, so it could go further.

'Twenty crates?' whispered Crutch. 'There are fifteen thousand people here.'

It was obvious Solokov had never been hungry. Arch Warden Gragor didn't look like he'd ever been short of food either.

'Those crates of food won't go far,' whispered Sergeant Zander.

'The people here can see that,' said Crutch. 'This won't go well.'

Crutch could see these people were starving. What would you do if your children were starving, close to death, and you could see food in front of you about to be given away, but you knew there wasn't enough to go around?

Solokov yelled, 'My magnificent gift to you. Come get food,' he said, motioning to the gallows platform.

The crowd surged forward. Screams from people desperate to get up the steps to the gallows mixed with the screams of the people at the front who were crushed and trampled.

'By the gods,' said Sergeant Zander. 'This will be worse than Zanithburg.'

Crutch remembered the crush of Estovians in Zanithburg. Being in it was terrifying. Having the breath crushed out of your lungs so you couldn't breathe. Trying to move but being completely helpless with your arms crushed to your sides.

Trapped, totally at the mercy of the crowd, pushing you backwards and forwards. Worse, seeing people next to you pushed helpless underneath the crowd and crushed to death.

Crutch didn't think it could get worse than Zanithburg, but watching the Estovians in People's Plaza was beyond horrible.

Many of the people were hungry and weak, and they folded under the push behind them, their faces pushed into the cobblestones and battered from above. Some didn't have the strength or the air left in them to scream, but those who did wailed and begged to be set free, yelled for people to please get off them.

Old women, old men, children, they were all being horribly crushed and trampled until the stones of the plaza became a bloody, pulpy mess. As the crowd rushed up the stairs to the stage, Gragor and his wardens fled through the solid wooden door at the back of the gallows.

More people climbed, and crawled, and flooded onto the wooden platform. People pushed and slid over the blood of the dead and injured to get onto the platform. Then the platform was so full of people, it became a killing zone, with Estovians pushed into the stone wall behind the gallows.

Those closest to the door Gragor and his wardens fled through tried to open it, but it was locked. They pounded on the door, screaming for someone to open it, as the life was pushed from their bodies.

As the crates of food disappeared under dead and crushed bodies, Solokov turned and walked off his speaking platform. Crutch and the marines left too, the screams and moans of the injured and dying ringing in their ears. There was nothing they could do to help here. They couldn't get to the people who needed help.

The path they took to get to Jasper later that day took them past the people's plaza. Komitav officers supervised Teevilgrad citizens, who hauled away the dead and scrubbed the blood off the cobblestones. Someone had painted the words *Igor's Kitchen* on the brick wall behind the gallows in blood, or what looked like blood. An old lady scrubbed at it under the direction of a komitav officer, but whatever it was, it wasn't coming off.

'Igor's gonna love that,' whispered Sergeant Zander.

Jasper sat dressed in an aquamarine-blue shimmering dress that only just went down below her crotch. She wore gold jewellery on her neck and gold earrings with pear centres. Her lips were painted a dark red.

'You were right,' said Crutch. 'Solokov did something worse.'

'I heard,' said Jasper. 'Your soup kitchen has him really worked up. How many people are you feeding?'

'Over ten thousand last night,' said Crutch.

'Impressive,' said Jasper, looking straight into Sergeant Zander's eyes.

'He tried to seize crates of food from the ships, but we still got more than enough to feed everyone,' said Crutch.

'And with all his money and resources, he doesn't give out any food and manages to kill a thousand Estovians,' said Jasper, still staring into Sergeant Zander's eyes. He stared right back.

'It's bigger than just the food. The people are coming together at the soup kitchen now, talking, dancing, making plans. There are so many of them; they're bringing chairs and filling up the hall and the street outside.'

'We need to get this key now, and you need to get the glowstone,' said Jasper. 'Whatever Solokov does next is likely to be horrible, almost beyond imagination.'

'You think so?' said Crutch. 'Trying to give away food isn't so horrible.'

'Solokov tried to give away food, but it failed terribly. He's arrogant and vain. He thinks it's impossible he could possibly have made a mistake or failed at anything. He'll revert to the methods that have worked for him in the past.'

'I'm afraid to ask what they are.'

'It will be ruthless and brutal', said Jasper. 'You should prepare the true compatriots to fight. They'll need that to have any chance of surviving.'

'What are their chances?' said Crutch. He'd started this, and now he was terrified he'd led another group of good people to their deaths like he had with those brave boys on the Kona Track at Papageenar.

'Ten thousand people might have a chance, if they fight. But they'd be up against Estovian army veterans and the loyal komitav. They're all trained, efficient killers.' Crutch thought of how hard it was to kill the one komitav officer who tried to rob him and imagined trying to fight hundreds of them. It would be a bloodbath.

'How long do you think we have?'

'Not long. A few days, maybe a week. But the longer it takes him to act next, the worse it will be. More time means he's building up to something bigger.'

'Do you know how to get the key to the vault the glowstone is in?' said Crutch.

'The komitav director has it,' said Jasper.

'How do we get to him?'

'I have a date with his magnificence, Director Uroslav, tomorrow night.'

'You have a date with him?' said Sergeant Zander.

'I do.'

'What kind of date?' said Sergeant Zander.

'The kind where you have dinner together, eat food, and then afterwards you, well, I'm sure you know how these things work, Sergeant Zander.'

'So you want us to kill him and take the key off him before he gets to the date?'

'Oh, Sergeant Zander. I do believe you're jealous.'

Sergeant Zander tried and failed to look like he didn't care.

'And you want to kill my suitor before he has a chance to hold my hand or kiss me,' said Jasper. 'How wonderfully barbaric you are.'

'Do you want us to kill him and get the key?' said Crutch.

'I thought you'd have a little more sophistication, Crutch. Seems you've been around Sergeant, hunk of muscle, Zander too long. Killing the komitav director and stealing the key would just make them add guards to the vault and change the lock.'

'So what do you have in mind?' said Crutch.

'Making a copy of the key.'

'How do we do that?' said Sergeant Zander.

'I need to get the key off him, then push it into a wax mould so I can cast the key later.'

'So what do you need us to do?' said Crutch.

'I need Sergeant Zander for his dashing looks, and I need you, Crutch, to take the key, push it into the wax mould, then give the key back to me.'

'Why don't you carry the wax mould yourself?' said Crutch.

'That would be perfect, but there is a problem. I won't be carrying anything in or out to my date, and my dress will be very tight.'

'You could wear something baggy,' said Sergeant Zander.

'Now you're being deliciously protective, Sergeant Zander. I don't think Director Uroslav will be too enthusiastic about the date if I'm wearing overalls.'

'How big is the mould?' said Crutch.

'Around twice the size of the key.'

'Could you strap it to your inside leg?'

'I like the way you think, Crutch, but I expect Director Uroslav to get quite handsy. That's how I intend to get the key.'

'I don't like this plan,' said Sergeant Zander.

'This is just wonderful,' said Jasper. 'I swear you're giving me tingles right now, Sergeant Zander.'

'So what's the plan?' said Crutch.

'I need Crutch to come down just above a balcony,' said Jasper. 'And I need you, Sergeant Zander, to lower him down.'

'Where is this balcony?' said Sergeant Zander.

'Just outside Director Uroslav's bedroom.'

'I think this is a terrible idea,' said Sergeant Zander. 'There must be another way that doesn't involve another man laying his hands on you.'

Jasper grabbed the back of Sergeant Zander's head and gave him a long, deep kiss. 'That is for being adorable.'

When she pulled away, Sergeant Zander stood there with his mouth open in surprise, then he pulled Jasper back in and kissed her right back.

CHAPTER 37
BROTHERS IN TRAINING

Sergeant Zander came with Crutch through the sewers to meet the Brothers of Mercy. They brought some soup and hard tack with them.

'Thank you for food,' said Torge. 'And thank you for sending Pavee with food every day. He is good boy.'

'You are welcome,' said Crutch. 'I bring friend with me. His name is Zanderth. Zanderth will show you how to fight komitav.'

'Is sad we need this training,' said Torge.

'I am ready to fight,' said Martov.

'One day you will understand that killing is not answer,' said Torge.

'They kill us, I kill them,' said Martov.

'And then we have war,' said Torge. 'Is sad.'

'Yes,' said Crutch. 'But for escape, we need your help. Need you to guard us while we get something important. Can you do this?'

'We will do,' said Torge.

'We may be attacked by komitav,' said Crutch. 'So training is important.'

'I understand,' said Torge.

'I hope komitav attack,' said Martov. 'I want to kill them all.'

'Enough,' said Torge. 'Brothers learn love not hate.'

'Sorry Torge,' said Martov.

Crutch gave verbal instructions while Sergeant Zander sparred with the Brothers of Mercy. Crutch wasn't confident Sergeant Zander could carry on a complex discussion without revealing his Ironborn accent. Jasper had taught them you were safest if no one knew who you were, and Crutch planned on keeping it that way.

'Komitav like to use feint when fighting in attack and defence,' said Crutch. 'Feint right, then attack left when using sword, or pretend to dodge left, then move other way when defending.'

Sergeant Zander went through some of the feints as Torge, Rohan, and Mortav took turns fighting against him.

'First time is dangerous,' said Crutch. 'But once you anticipate feint, you can pretend it works, then attack hard knowing what to expect.'

The Brothers of Mercy picked up on the fighting patterns very fast. Sergeant Zander smiled each time he launched an attack after a feint. Just one time seeing the feint, and they were never fooled again. Torge wasn't even fooled the first time.

'You are all good,' said Sergeant Zander.

'Zanderth can train with you for next two hours,' said Crutch.

'Is not necessary,' said Torge. 'We have seen now. We can train with each other. Find our own ways to fight komitav.'

Crutch smiled. 'Then time for soup?'

'Yes,' said Torge.

They sat and talked together as they ate. Sergeant Zander just nodded and smiled without saying anything.

'When you escape, what will you do?' said Crutch.

'Find land. Grow food.'

'So you need to find farm, find good land?' said Crutch.

'Brothers of Mercy don't need good land to farm,' said Torge. 'Can farm on nearly anything.'

'Really?'

'Yes. Old secret. Use legume trees in bad soil. Then soil improves, can use piles of leaves from legume trees, and grow yam vines up trees. Then tree roots and yam drive down into hard soil. Harvest yam, then grow sweet potato.'

'Why don't Estovians grow this way?'

'Estovians don't like to eat beans from trees. Don't like taste.'

'Don't like taste?'

'How do they put it? 'Taste like sloppy dog turd.' Won't eat them.'

'I know some people who will eat them,' said Crutch. 'Can you turn tree beans into beer?'

'Not exactly beer, but can make alcoholic drink. We call it volktag.'

Crutch smiled. 'Is good. Gives me idea.'

Chapter 38
The Seeds Of Rebellion

That night, Andreas the minstrel brought another man in his fifties up to Crutch.

'This is Crujge,' said Andreas. 'Crujge, this is my friend, great percussionist Kareli Bureeva.'

'I play best percussion in whole of Teevilgrad in exchange for soup.'

'Welcome to soup kitchen,' said Crutch. 'Love to hear you play, but soup is free. Don't have to play.'

'Soup is free?' said Kareli.

'Free,' said Crutch.

'You are all wonderful people,' said Kareli. The people working in the kitchen looked up and smiled. 'Wonderful, wonderful people.'

As they went to join the line, Andreas said, 'See, I told you soup is free.'

'You tell me, but I don't believe it. Wonderful people.'

When people had finished eating their soup, they gathered in the hall and on the street. Crutch didn't think it was possible, but the number of people coming to the soup kitchen had grown even more. Crutch estimated that they fed nearly twenty thousand people that night once you added in the people who brought in pots to take soup home to their families and friends who couldn't get to the soup kitchen.

The street outside the hall was full of chairs, and people standing and talking. There was an energy now, like a buzz that went through the whole crowd. This went way beyond eating. People were talking about change, and new beginnings, and lives without war and hunger.

And they started talking about lives without Emporer Solokov. Crutch felt a fear inside at that. This was what he came to Teevilgrad to do. To sow the seeds of rebellion. But he'd fallen in love with these people, these true compatriots, who only wanted a better life for themselves and their children.

He knew the time was coming they'd have to pay for that better life in blood, and the chances were, even with their blood spilled on the streets of Teevilgrad, Igor Solokov would make sure that better life never came.

Sergeant Zander spent more time at the soup kitchen and was familiar with many of the regulars now. They knew he helped drive the wagon to get food from the docks. Being one of the very few men under fifty, he was very popular with the ladies. He would avoid talking to them and escape to the storage room off the kitchen if they got too enthusiastic with their advances.

But the one thing Sergeant Zander loved was the dancing.

The first notes of Andreas on his now-familiar stringed instrument rang out. The floor of the hall cleared, and a huge circle of people formed to dance. Kareli had a long, heavy stick with leather tied to the end of it. He banged on the floor in time with Andreas.

A large circle of dancers formed. People in the hall and out in the street clapped and yelled in time as they watched the dancers. There was a magic in the music, like all the people were lifting each other up and spinning them around, flinging off their troubles and losing themselves in a dance of joy.

In between songs, Anton and Yelena waved for Crutch to come join them. Crutch shook his head, no. Anton waved him over again, and Crutch shook his head no again. Anton walked over to him.

'Come dance with us,' he said.
'I can't,' said Crutch. 'I am too old and my leg.'
'Is alright,' said Anton. 'You can lean on me.'
Anton grabbed his hand and led him out to join the circle.

'You won't need cane,' said Anton, so Crutch slid it into his belt. Anton and Yelena smiled as Crutch put his left arm on Anton and his right arm on Yelena.

Andreas started playing, and Anton said, 'Lean on me every second step. I am just like walking cane.'

It was awkward at first. Crutch didn't know how to move his feet, and he stumbled, but Anton held him firm with his arm so he couldn't fall. Andreas watched him and took as much time as he could, playing at the slowest pace.

By the time Andreas began to speed up, Crutch had the steps down and was enjoying himself. Anton and Yelena were smiling at him and laughing. When he looked around the circle of people dancing with him, he saw joy on the faces of the dancers. Outside the circle, it felt like the people clapping and yelling were lifting him on wings.

For the first time in his life, it felt like his weak leg didn't matter, like he could dance and move as long as he was here with the people who lifted him up with their spirit, with their love.

The music was in full swing when Arch Warden Gragor marched through the entrance, pushing past the people there. He marched to the centre of the hall with his five wardens behind him and yelled, 'Stop the music!'

Andreas stopped and looked up in surprise, his toothless mouth open.

Some of the people kept clapping in time, and a few people kept dancing.

'Silence!' yelled Gragor.

The room fell still.

'There will be no more dancing!'

Murmurs went around the hall. People turned and looked at each other in confusion, not understanding what was going on.

The old lady, Leena, walked up to Arch Warden Gragor. 'Is just dancing. You will like if you try.'

Gragor stared at her.

'Your ma never taught you to dance,' said Leena. 'Look, I show you.'

Anton's face went pale. 'No Leena.'

'Is alright, Anton. Arch Warden Gragor just needs to learn steps. Is easy. Step right first, just like walking, except sideways see. Then, when everyone yells out you change and step left.'

Andreas started playing again, with Kareli pounding his stick on the floor. Everyone started clapping and yelling as Leena hobbled to the right, then the left.

'If old woman like me can do, you can do too.'

Anton tried to yell, 'Stop!' but the sound of clapping and yelling drowned out his voice.

Crutch hobbled in to get to Leena, to pull her away, do something to stop this. But he was too late.

Gragor backhanded Leena across the face, her old body crumpling on the floor.

'Stop dancing!' Gragor yelled.

Silence fell in the hall and on the street outside. Monika hobbled to Leena's side and knelt down beside her limp body. She stared up at Gragor and said, 'You are disgusting animal!'

Gragor shook with anger and pulled his hand back, ready to hit her, then he stopped.

'By order of his magnificence, the Emperor Igor Solokov, there will be no more dancing!' Gragor looked directly at Anton. 'Control your people, Anton, or they will all be hanging in People's Plaza.'

'And no music!' Gragor walked over to Andreas, grabbed his instrument, smashed it over his knee, and threw it to the floor. Gragor looked at Kareli's stick, thought better of it, then he and his wardens marched out.

Chapter 39
The Key

Crutch and Sergeant Zander left soon after Arch Warden Gragor had stopped the dancing at the soup kitchen. Tonight they had to help Jasper get the komitav director's key.

The komitav director's mansion was between the palace and the Komitav Operative building. The bottom floor had two guards at the entrance, but it seemed obvious that no one expected any trouble. That made sense to Crutch. If there was trouble, they could call on the komitav officers just a block away. They could call the palace guards too.

Crutch and Sergeant Zander had already checked the building and seen a way to climb up the side. They made sure the guards weren't anywhere near them and quietly climbed up the wall, using the cracks in the large stone bricks and beams as footholds. It was challenging, but after climbing in the rigging of a ship, it was well within Crutch's skill level.

It was high when they finally got to the roof, probably thirty feet up. Crutch looked out and could see the top of the komitav operative building. Solokov's palace still towered over them. Nothing was higher or larger than the palace.

They crept across the roof until they found the bedroom balcony.

'I still think I should be the one on the rope,' whispered Sergeant Zander.

'We've been through this,' whispered Crutch. 'I can't hold your weight.'

'I could climb down.'

'You need to be hanging upside down so Jasper can pass you the key. It has to be me on the rope.'

Crutch figured Sergeant Zander just wanted to get a look at what was going on inside the director's bedroom with Jasper. He got the feeling if the sergeant did see what was going on, he might try to do something to stop it, then they'd be fighting off the entire Komitav Operative.

From the roof to the bedroom balcony was at least ten feet. As Sergeant Zander lowered him down, Crutch could see the balcony had glass doors. Crutch would have to go down just far enough so he could reach Jasper passing him the key as she came to the door. Then, while hanging upside down, he had to get out the wax mould, press the key into it, and pass it back down to Jasper.

And they had to do it all without the director noticing, even though he was likely to be right next to Jasper when they made the pass of the key back and forth. If the director saw him, their only chance would be to try to escape over the roofs, but their chances of getting away would be slim once an alert was sounded.

Crutch went down till his head was just above the upper edge of the glass doors. He signalled Sergeant Zander to stop. He jerked to a halt as Sergeant Zander stopped lowering the rope around his legs. Crutch listened. He could hear two voices: Jasper and a man.

'You so strong,' said Jasper. 'Must train hard like powerful warrior.'

'Once. When I was younger,' said the director.

'I like to feel such huge muscles.'

'You can feel as much as you want.'

'You have other muscle I can feel.'

Crutch dropped like a stone to the balcony, barely getting his hands out in time so he didn't land on his head. He lay as flat as he could, looked up at Sergeant Zander, and motioned frantically to get him to pull him up. Crutch looked inside. Had the director seen him? Were they about to be overrun by every guard from the Komitav Operative?

Jasper saw Crutch lying on the balcony, kissed the director, and spun him so he faced away from Crutch. While they kissed, Jasper had her eyes on Crutch. With her hand behind the director's body, she motioned for him to go up. He was trying.

He felt a tug on the rope around his legs, then he went up, spinning round as he went. He saw the lights of Teevilgrad below the mansion, then spun around and saw Jasper kissing the director, watching him go up. Then he was above the glass doors again and used his hands on the wall to stop his body from spinning.

After his heart calmed, Crutch focused on the voices inside.'

'I tell you what I love,' said Jasper.

'What you love?' said the director.

'I love those blue sugar plums. Make me so hot, if you know what I mean?'

The rope around his legs shook, and Crutch dropped a few inches. He glared up at Sergeant Zander, who looked back and mouthed, 'Sorry.'

'I do. I do know what you mean,' said the director. 'Stay here. I get guard to bring.'

'Oh, director Uroslav. You are such powerful man.'

Crutch could hear Jasper's footsteps getting closer to the glass doors. The door opened just a fraction, and he could see her hands and the key coming through the crack. He reached down, but the key was just out of his reach. He motioned for Sergeant Zander to lower him. He dropped a few inches, then he had the key.

Crutch opened the mould tied to his waist and carefully pushed the key into it, making sure it was fully in. Then he pulled out the key and closed the mould case. It was time to get the key back to Jasper, but the glass door was closed. Where was she? He listened for the voices below.

'Will only take five minutes,' said the director.

'Five minutes. Oh my. So quick. I bet not everything you do so quick.'

'You bet right,' said the director.

Crutch shook again as the rope around his legs went loose for a fraction of a second, then tight again. Crutch figured it would be five minutes until Jasper had another chance to get to the glass doors so he could pass the key back. He was already feeling woozy from hanging upside down. Getting dropped onto the balcony didn't help either. He signalled for Sergeant Zander to pull him up.

'Did you do the swap?' whispered Sergeant Zander.

'I got the key and got it into the mould. Still have to give Jasper the key back. Give it a few minutes. What happened to you?' whispered Crutch.

'I could hear Jasper's voice echoing through the roof,' whispered Sergeant Zander. 'It distracted me.'

'You could have got us all killed, including Jasper.'

When he said that, Sergeant Zander looked like he'd been punched.

'Sorry.'

They waited in silence for a couple of minutes. Sergeant Zander had said he'd heard Jasper's voice from here, but right now they couldn't hear anything.

'Lower me back down,' said Crutch.

For a second, Sergeant Zander lowered him a bit too far, and Crutch could see why there were no voices. Jasper and the director were in a passionate embrace. Crutch was glad Sergeant Zander couldn't see this. He motioned for Sergeant Zander to pull him up a little and waited, listening.

There was a knock on the door of the bedroom.

'Go away,' yelled the director.

'Might be sugar plums,' said Jasper. 'I love sugar plums.'

'Then you will get,' said the director.

Crutch heard footsteps coming towards the glass door again. He leaned down with the key in his hand, ready to pass it back to Jasper. He saw the door crack open, and it hit his hand and flung the key onto the balcony. The key was right on the edge, with half of it hanging off. If it fell off the balcony, they were in serious trouble.

'I have your sugar plums,' said the director.

The glass door closed, and Crutch could hear her footsteps going back towards the director in the room.

'You know just how to treat lady,' said Jasper.

Crutch could see the key, but he couldn't go down and get it while there was a chance the director could see.

'Open mouth. I have sugar plum for you.'

'So romantic,' said Jasper. 'Mm is delicious. I can think of something else delicious.'

'I like way you think.'

The rope around Crutch's legs started trembling.

153

'Come over here with me against wall,' said Jasper. 'Only want to see your handsome face.'

Was that code? Crutch signalled for Sergeant Zander to lower him down a little. Just enough so he could see. Jasper had her back against the wall, with the director kissing her. Behind his back, she signalled for him to get the key.

Crutch signalled to Sergeant Zander to drop him to the balcony. He tried to land as soft and quiet as he could. Crutch crawled towards the key, keeping his eyes on Jasper and the director behind him. Just as he was about to grab it he saw the director starting to turn towards him.

And he knocked the key with the fingertips of his left hand, and saw it slipping over the edge of the balcony.

And caught it in the air with his right hand.

He signalled for Sergeant Zander to haul him up fast. Crutch could see the director still turning slowly as Jasper tried to pull him back around.

Crutch had another problem. He was going up fast, but the top of his body now swung towards the glass doors of the balcony. He put out his hands, but he hit the doors hard, cracking the glass on one of them before Sergeant Zander hauled him up to the roof.

Now he could hear the voices echoing through the roof.

'What was that?' said the director.

'Oh my goodness,' said Jasper. 'Bird flew into glass door.'

'Bird?' said the director.

'Big bird. Then it fell down on balcony and flew off.'

Jasper appeared out of the balcony door, looking up for just and instant mouthing, 'Drop,' then pointing with a finger to her open right palm. Then her hands were down as the director was on the balcony.

'Must be big bird,' said the director, looking at the crack in the glass.

'Was big,' said Jasper, putting her arms around the director's neck. 'But not as big as you.'

'You like?'

'I like,' said Jasper. 'Can fix glass later. Have better things to do now.'

Sergeant Zander had his dagger out. Crutch grabbed the wrist of Sergeant Zander's dagger hand and pushed it down.

The director pulled away and grabbed Jasper's left hand. He started pulling her back through the open glass doors. As the director pulled her away, Jasper held out her right palm behind her. Crutch saw it and knew exactly what she wanted. *Just one chance.*

He dropped the key, and it landed perfectly in Jasper's palm before she disappeared inside the bedroom.

Crutch took a deep breath. Sergeant Zander looked like he was taking a giant turd, but the turd was stuck and wouldn't come out.

'We should kill him.'

'That will get us all killed,' said Crutch. 'We need to go.'

Sergeant Zander looked down at the balcony, his hands shaking with anger.

'Now,' whispered Crutch.

Chapter 40
The Dance Of War

Before the people started turning up to eat at the soup kitchen, Crutch had a chance to talk to Anton.

'Was bad thing last night,' said Crutch.

'Worse than you think,' said Anton. 'The wardens are Solokov's most loyal brutal killers. They do worst work for emperor. Arch Warden Gragor is bad man.'

'I thought he was komitav.'

'Yes, but special komitav. Most komitav hate him.'

'Is Leena okay?'

'I checked on her,' said Anton. 'Is okay. Will be in tonight.'

'Am happy to hear that,' said Crutch. 'Is wrong.'

'Solokov wants to stop dancing,' said Anton. 'Wants to stop soup kitchen because it makes him look bad. Doesn't care people will starve.'

'What will you do, Anton? If Solokov tries to close soup kitchen.'

'Only one thing we can do. We will fight.'

'Is dangerous,' said Crutch. 'Many true compatriots could die.'

'Before you come, they starve to death. Better to die fighting than die from hunger. Will not let them close soup kitchen.'

'You are brave man,' said Crutch. 'Wish more men like you.'

'Plenty like me here,' said Anton. 'Enough to stop Solokov.'

'I hope so,' said Crutch.

Crutch had always been with the marines or soldiers in those hours before a major battle when you're strung tight, knowing the fight was about to come. He'd never been with women and old men.

But that was the feeling at the soup kitchen the night after Arch Warden Gragor ordered the True Compatriots to stop dancing. The air hummed with malice mixed and a grinding anticipation. People who'd seen Leena get hit were quiet, but Crutch could tell they were seething with anger.

Yelena served the soup with kind smiles, but when she worked, she cut the vegetables like they were Emperor Solokov's private parts. In the kitchen, the energy was the same for everyone working there.

If Gragor walked in now, Crutch was sure they would have torn him to pieces with their teeth and their fingernails, just like the Papageenan women did to the Estovians on the Kona Track.

The turnout for soup was the largest ever, and the number of people who stayed after they'd eaten was larger still. People packed the hall and the street so tight only the oldest had chairs. People who brought chairs left them in the side streets and stood, packed together, the talk angry and defiant.

Andreas had taken the strings from his broken instrument and nailed them to an old plank of wood. Kareli sat right there with him, his stick ready. When Andreas started playing, the strings jangled and hummed rough against the wood plank, but it was enough for the people in the hall to pick up the rhythm and start clapping and yelling. Andreas smiled his toothless smile as the clapping grew louder, then his face turned to furious concentration.

Leena hobbled to the centre of the hall. Crutch could see her split lip and an ugly bruise on her face from Arch Warden Gragor's attack. In her old, throaty voice, she yelled, 'No one can tell me not to dance! Fuck Igor!'

The people in the hall and on the street applauded furiously. Chants of 'Fuck Igor!' rang around the hall. Leena danced by herself for a minute as the hall and street erupted in cheers of encouragement, then other dancers joined her, forming a circle of defiance.

They danced with a mix of joy and anger. They stepped so hard on the wooden floor, Crutch could hear the pounding shaking the floor over the music and the clapping.

'I can't stop them,' said Anton.

'Nothing can stop them,' said Crutch.

'I don't want to stop them.'

'Neither do I.'

Anton took Yelena by the hand, and they joined the circle of dancers to the cheers of everyone in the hall and on the street. Crutch watched them dance, pounding every step as if they were pounding into Igor Solokov's face. They danced with anger, with determination, spines erect and eyes staring forward, staring down the enemy, daring him to attack. This was the dance of war.

Sergeant Zander moved among the true compatriots. Anyone he thought might be able to fight, he'd give a spear head.

'Attach to broom handle. Make spear to defend yourself.'

Crutch knew this was no longer just a soup kitchen. It started with the cooking of soup and the feeding of a few street urchins, but now rebellion was brewing and the true compatriots hall was its heart.

Crutch saw the thousands of people in the hall and out in the street. Maybe there were enough now that Solokov would think twice about trying to stop them. Maybe they could find a way out of this that didn't mean bloodshed.

He looked at Sergeant Zander handing out spear heads and the look on the faces of the people who took them. That look of satisfaction and determination showed that not only were they ready to fight but now they had something to fight with.

There would be blood.

Chapter 41
Discussing Politics

They met Jasper in the same tavern the next day. Jasper was in a short red skirt and a sheer pink blouse. Every time she looked at Sergeant Zander, he looked away, guilt plastered on his face.

She led them upstairs with Sergeant Zander's eyes fixed on every step she made. Once they got to the room, Crutch gave her the mould he'd made with the komitav director's key, and Jasper poured some kind of liquid metal into it.

'Needs filling right up,' said Jasper, 'to get complete satisfaction.'

'You mean to make the key,' said Crutch.

'Maybe,' said Jasper.

'Now we just wait for it to get hard.' She looked at Sergeant Zander, and he looked away again. She moved his chin with her finger until he looked right at her, smiled, then continued her work on making the key.

'Now we let chemistry take its course,' said Jasper, looking at Sergeant Zander who stared back at her. 'Do you have a plan for getting the glowstone now you have the key?'

'We're working on it,' said Crutch.

'Get it done soon,' said Jasper. I'd like to be more help, but I'm leaving Teevilgrad tonight.'

Sergeant Zander's face dropped.

Jasper pulled the finished key out of the mould.

'And there's your key. Nice and hard, just the way I like it.'

'Thank you, Jasper,' said Crutch. 'Thank you for everything.'

'I wish you the best of luck and hope to see you both again in Ironbay, if by some miracle you make it back alive.'

Crutch turned to leave. Sergeant Zander was still staring at Jasper.

'I don't leave for three hours, Sergeant Zander if you'd like to stay a while and discuss, I don't know, politics?'

'Yes. Yes, I would,' said Sergeant Zander. 'Politics is my favourite topic.'

'Sergeant Zander will catch you up a little later,' said Jasper. 'We need to discuss the interplay between agricultural trade and military protection in the territories.'

'It could take a while,' said Sergeant Zander.

Crutch closed the door as Jasper and Sergeant Zander started to kiss.

Chapter 42
Where Is Crujge?

It was nearly an hour before dawn when Arch Warden Gragor entered the inn Crutch and the marines stayed at. He had his five wardens with him, fully armed with weapons drawn. Behind him were another dozen komitav officers. At the steps to the alley entrance were another twenty komitav officers.

They moved silently, opening the first door to the basement steps at the front, then going down the steps to the second door. Gragor motioned for one of his wardens to pick the door lock. The warden had it unlocked in seconds. Two wardens with swords pushed them through the cracks in the door, then up to take off the bar.

The wardens flung the door open, then spread out into the room away from the door so the komitav officers behind them with crossbows would have a clear shot into the room.

The wardens stopped and looked. Then they looked for any hidden doors, hidden nooks, or hidden exits. There were none.

Except for a single wooden crate, the room was completely empty.

Gragor kicked the crate across the room, where it smashed into pieces in a wall.

'Where is Crujge?' he yelled in frustration.

Crutch and the marines sat in the sewers, trying to stay on the drier stones. That was difficult to do in the dark.

'When Sergeant Zander put you in charge of finding our accommodation for this mission, I was a bit worried,' said Longshot. 'But you've outdone yourself this time.'

'Would have been easier if you didn't have so many sacks,' said Crutch. He looked around. Each of them had to lug two or three sacks from the inn.

'Quicksilver and I kept ourselves busy,' said Longshot.

'Does Anton know why Arch Warden Gragor was hunting us?' said Quicksilver.

'He didn't have details,' said Crutch. 'All he knew was that we were on some kind of list.'

'You think Solokov is after everyone running the soup kitchen?' said Longshot.

'That's possible, but I hope not,' said Crutch. 'He could be after me because I was buying food through Inspector Petrov at the docks. Or Solokov might have spies who saw me somewhere else, like one of those taverns where Sergeant Zander and I were getting the young sailors and soldiers worked up.'

'Either way, Crutch can't move freely in Teevilburg any more,' said Sergeant Zander. 'We need to get all this gear where we need it in the sewers before dawn. We go for the glowstone tomorrow night.'

'I've been looking forward to this,' said Quicksilver. 'Do I get to set things on fire now?'

'You do,' said Sergeant Zander.

'Thank the gods.'

They hid in the sewers most of the day, munching on hard tack and quietly going through their plans. Above them, Teevilgrad was humming. Around ten in the morning, they heard the first announcement. They could hear a crier ringing a bell moving down the street.

'Five o'clock. His magnificence, Emperor Solokov, speaks in People's Plaza. All able-bodied should attend.'

'What is that about?' said Sergeant Zander.

'I don't know, but knowing Solokov, it won't be good for someone.'

CHAPTER 43
ENEMY OF THE PEOPLE

Crutch and the marines had been in Teevilgrad too long to let it go. They had to see what Emperor Solokov would do next. They hid in the shadows of an alley across the street from the People's Plaza. The plaza was packed full of people, even more than the last time when hundreds of them died in a crush.

Crutch could just make out the words Igor's Kitchen painted in red on the brick wall behind the gallows platform. It was faded, like someone had scrubbed at it over and over, but you could still read it.

There was a new addition in the People's Plaza. A strong chest-high fence made of metal bars between the gallows platform and the crowd. People could still get crushed to death, but Solokov's wardens on the gallows platform should be safe. How comforting.

'Maybe he's starting soup kitchens all over Teevilgrad,' whispered Quicksilver. 'It worked to get Anton a huge following. I always say fight fire with fire.'

'You always say fight everything with fire,' whispered Longshot.

Quicksilver grinned.

Crutch hoped somewhere in his heart that Solokov had decided to try feeding the people of Teevilgrad instead of crushing them under his boot. They had proved it could work with the soup kitchen. But much more likely, what he did today would be the start of him reasserting his authority, most likely in a cruel and brutal way.

He looked in the crowd. He recognised some of the people from the soup kitchen. What was more interesting was that, even though he must have seen at least twenty thousand different people go through the soup kitchen, he didn't recognise most of the people here. There were a lot of people in Teevilgrad.

There was a murmur in the crowd, an energy like the way the air felt when you were on the ocean, and a lightning storm was coming. It was the same as last night in the true compatriots hall.

'They're ready to fight,' whispered Crutch.

Sergeant Zander looked at them. 'You're right. Some of them are holding weapons too, under their clothes.'

Crutch squinted his eyes and really looked at the people closest to him. Sergeant Zander was right. He could see women with knives hidden in the pockets of their skirts, the outlines barely visible. Kitchen knives, most likely.

There was an old man who had his hand under a light jacket. From the side, Crutch could just see it. A spear with the handle snapped in half so it could be concealed. A short spear would kill you just as dead as a long spear, especially if someone stuck you from behind with it.

He wondered how many of the people here were carrying spears made from the spear heads Sergeant Zander gave them at the soup kitchen.

Now he'd seen it, he couldn't unsee it. Every second or third person hid something they could fight with. He saw the outline of a frying pan under the back of one woman's skirt; another had a rolling pin under her blouse.

'What do these people plan on doing?' whispered Crutch.

'Rebellions don't start with a plan,' whispered Sergeant Zander. 'They start with anger that boils over and a lot of blood.'

A horn sounded, and angry murmurs went through the crowd.

'Hail his magnificence, Emperor Igor Solokov.'

Solokov stepped out onto his platform in view of the crowd with his gold robes and his red sash. Hisses and boos rose up. From where they were standing, Crutch could feel the anger and the hate boiling in the people on the plaza.

'My people,' yelled Solokov over the booing. 'Is difficult time. I know sometimes you hungry. Not enough to eat. Same for me.'

That brought even louder boos.

'Not same for you. My baby died,' yelled one woman.

'You feed your poodles more than you feed us.'

'When have you ever gone hungry?'

Solokov kept talking. It was like he had no idea what a slimy sack of dog turd he really was. As if he expected the people of Teevilgrad to love him while he got fat and they starved.

'I find reason you hungry. Group who call themselves true compatriots really traitors and puppets of Ironbay. Make fake soup kitchen to steal your food so you starve. Send food to Ironbay on ships.'

Arch warden Gragor appeared through the door behind the gallows, pushing a woman whose wrists were bound ahead of him. Leena. She turned and spat in his face. He returned the favour by punching her so hard she fell to the boards of the gallows platform, hitting them hard on her stomach. Gragor grabbed her by the arms and yanked her back up to her feet.

Wardens brought other people through the door. Andreas the musician, his friend Kareli, and Leena's friend Monkia. The last two wardens brought out two boys, Dima and his friend Tamiva.

'Bastard,' whispered Sergeant Zander.

The crowd hissed and yelled.

'True compatriots only ones who help.'

'You want to hang old women and young boys now. So brave, Igor.'

'You greedy pig, Igor.'

Solokov yelled to get his voice over the noise of the crowd. 'These traitors and enemies of Teevilgrad must die. All true compatriots must die,' he yelled.

Crutch couldn't stand there and watch this. Without thinking, he was already across the road. He pushed through the crowd of people, but they were packed tight, and he barely made progress forward. Sergeant Zander and the marines were behind him.

As Arch Warden Gragor put the noose around Leena's neck, she yelled, 'Fuck Igor!'

Dima yelled out, 'Has too much, still wants more. Ee ore, ee ore, fat pig Igor!' Tamiva joined in with the second half of the nursery rhyme as a warden tightened the noose around his neck.

Andreas stood proud and defiant with a noose around his neck and yelled, 'Fuck Igor, fuck Igor,' in a slow rhythm over and over. A chant started from the crowd. Karili, Leena, Tamiva, and Dima joined in. Brave and proud to the end.

Crutch tried to push through the crowd, to get to the gallows, but they were packed tight and pushing back. He and the marines had only managed to get twenty yards from the edge of the crowd.

Solokov raised his sword as the crowd chanted 'Fuck Igor,' over and over, so loud his ears were ringing from the sound.

Solokov yelled, 'Victory for all,' and dropped his sword.

And they dropped. Leena's body jerked at the end of the rope, then stopped. Crutch could see no reason why Solokov thought killing an old woman would help his cause. Monika, Andreas, Kareli and Dima were all wonderful, kind people who gave so much to the people around them. To Teevilgrad. Now they were just lifeless corpses on the end of a rope.

Tamiva still kicked his legs, hanging at the end of the rope. Crutch's knees went weak as he looked on in horror. This was One-eye on the gallows in Ironbay all over again. Tamiva wasn't heavy enough to break his neck in the fall. One-eye had hung for twenty minutes, choking on the gallows at Ironbay, until he finally stopped moving.

Arch Warden Gragor looked over and saw Tamiva kicking. He walked over, leaned in, and grabbed Tamiva by the hair, drew a dagger, lifted him up, and cut through his neck with one brutal slash. He cut so hard and deep the head came off. Tamiva's lifeless body dropped through the hole in the gallows platform. On the way down, it slapped against the trap door, leaving it swinging.

Crutch looked up at Emperor Solokov and realised Solokov was looking straight back at him. In that moment, Crutch knew deep in his soul. He knew that war would never end until Solokov was dead and buried.

Anger swelled through the crowd. If Solokov thought killing old women and children would terrify the people of Teevilgad into submission, he was very wrong.

The crowd pushed forward against the fence of iron bars, yelling and cursing. One man threw a short spear straight at Solokov, missing his face by inches. Solokov ran off the platform.

'Run you coward.'

The fence began to buckle as the crowd pushed forward, their angry yelling now as loud as rolling thunder.

Arch Warden Gragor and his five wardens fled through the door at the back of the gallows, leaving the corpses of the true compatriots spinning behind them.

'We have to go now,' said Sergeant Zander.

'To the palace!' yelled someone in the crowd.

'Kill Igor. To the palace!' yelled another. The crowd began to move out of the People's Plaza, pushing Crutch and the marines with them.

They broke off and headed across the street and down the alley, away from the crowd.

The sun set on the crowd of people behind them marching for the palace and on any hopes Crutch had that they might leave Teevilgrad a better place.

Chapter 44
Horse And Wagon

'With the people storming the palace, what do you think Solokov will do?' said Sergeant Zander.

'He's a coward. He'll mobilise his army and the komitav to protect him,' said Crutch.

'That means the Komitav Operative will be almost empty,' said Sergeant Zander.

'Gotta love it when a plan comes together,' said Crutch with an edge of bitterness. They just paved the way for their best chance of getting the glowstone, but at what cost? Innocent civilians who just wanted to eat and live with a little dignity, now fighting for their survival.

'If we're the enemy of the people, what will happen to the true compatriots hall,' said Crutch.

'Nothing good,' said Sergeant Zander.

'We need the horse, wagon, barrels, and sacks to carry the glowstone,' said Crutch.

'It's dark enough. We'll go there now,' said Sergeant Zander. 'Through the sewers.'

'The sewers?' said Quicksilver.

'Solokov will be looking for all the true compatriots,' said Sergeant Zander. 'That includes Crutch, me, and Boulder. We don't want to be seen.'

'So we're wading through the sewers again,' said Quicksilver.

'Exactly.'

'Being an enemy of the people is a pain in the arse.'

They smelled the smoke and felt the heat of the fire long before they got to the hall. When Crutch looked out of the sewer grate at the true compatriots hall, it was on fire, burning fiercely.

Crutch could see some true compatriots standing across the road with tears in their eyes.

'Like we thought. It's on fire,' said Crutch. The stables with the horse and wagon were in a building next door to the hall.

Quicksilver pushed his way next to Crutch to take a look.

'Nice fire!' he said.

'There's still a chance we can get the horse and wagon,' said Sergeant Zander. 'Let's hope we're not too late.

They ran through the sewers as best they could, heading for the stables. They could feel the heat of the fire above them radiating through the stones over their heads. Boulder had to crouch down as he ran to avoid banging his head.

There was no one in the alley when Crutch got to the grate. He looked out, and the stables weren't burned, but the fire from the hall burning next to it was getting closer. Sparks were jumping in the air, dropping on the stones of the alley. It was just a matter of time before the stable was set alight.

'Let's get up there,' said Sergeant Zander.

Crutch pushed the sewer grate off and climbed out with the other marines close behind. They ran down the alley to the doors of the stable. Crutch looked inside, and the horse was there, unsettled by the smell of smoke and the intense heat coming from the fire in the hall just a few yards away.

'We'll have to be careful and keep a good hold on the horse,' said Sergeant Zander. 'It could shy and gallop away from us when it sees how big that fire is.'

'I'll do it,' said Longshot. 'I'm good with horses.'

Sparks fell onto Crutch's back. One burned through his shirt and into his neck. As Longshot opened the stable doors enough to squeeze through, Crutch looked at the hay on the floor of the stables. One spark would set that hay on fire, and sparks were falling everywhere.

Longshot took hold of the horse, put a bridle on it, and led it to the front of the wagon. The wagon was already loaded with empty barrels and sacks, as they'd done every night. Longshot just got the horse hitched to the wagon when a spark blew through the barred window in the stable doors and landed on the hay.

With the heat from next door, the hay was bone dry, and it immediately burst into flames. Sergeant Zander threw open the barn doors and ran for the horse. Crutch and the other marines were right behind him. The horse reared up on its hind legs, fear in its eyes, and the flames grew.

Crutch grabbed a sack from the wagon and pounded at the flames closest to the horse, trying to belt them down to clear a way.

Longshot and Sergeant Zander were talking softly to the horse, stroking it, trying to calm it down. The fire in the hay made more sparks, and they flew onto the walls and into the rafters of the stable.

'We have to go now,' said Sergeant Zander. 'Get in the wagon, Crutch.'

Crutch climbed up to the wagon seat, and Sergeant Zander gave him the reins.

'Hold those tight and rein in the horse hard, or he'll gallop and you and the wagon will smash on the first corner,' said Sergeant Zander.

'Bits of fire dropped from the rafters onto Crutch. The horse made terrified sounds and kicked at the ground.

Sergeant Zander went back and held the horse's bridle on one side while Longshot held it on the other. Boulder and Quicksilver were keeping the flames off the barrels and the sacks on the back of the wagon the best they could.

Crutch felt like he was burning as Sergeant Zander and Longshot led the horse out of the barn doors over the burning hay at a steady walk, as calmly as they could. Crutch could smell singed hair. He didn't know if it was his, or Sergeant Zander's, or the horse's. He knew that he was getting burned. They were all getting burned.

'He's likely to try to kick off now when we walk past the fire,' said Sergeant Zander in a calm, steady voice.

'It's okay,' said Longshot to the horse. 'It's okay.'

As they walked down the alley, the hall next to them roared with flames. They kept going as far down the alley as they could until they were away from the fire.

'We have to get this horse and wagon near the Komitav Directive building. Somewhere safe, where we can stash them until we need them tonight.'

Crutch and the marines had checked out all the buildings near the Komitav Directive looking for a way in. One place seemed perfect for it.

'What about the abandoned warehouses two blocks over,' said Crutch. 'The iron works.'

'That should work,' said Sergeant Zander. 'We go that way.'

'Still have to get there without being caught by Solokov's men,' said Crutch.

'The good news is most of them will be at the palace.'

They led the horse and wagon down side streets as far as they could. Longshot poured water into his hand from his waterskin to give the horse every time they paused to make sure the next street or alley they were going down was clear. They knew they'd have to cross the main street, and they knew that was their biggest chance of being discovered.

When they came to the main street, Crutch, Sergeant Zander, and Quicksilver went to the corner and looked both ways. One end of the street looked clear. There were komitav and civilians further down the other end of the street at a distance.

'Are they fighting?' said Crutch.

'Could be,' said Sergeant Zander. 'Hard to tell from this distance.'

Quicksilver came to their side. 'I say we make a run for it across the road while they're distracted fighting each other.'

'Don't have too many other choices,' said Sergeant Zander.

They went back to Longshot. Crutch climbed back up onto the wagon seat and took the reins.

'On three, you go across the street full gallop,' said Sergeant Zander. 'We'll run behind.'

Crutch nodded.

'One,' said Sergeant Zander.

Crutch braced his feet against the footboard. Going full gallop on a cobblestone street would be a wild ride.

'Two.'

Crutch could hear the sound of the civilians and the komitav getting closer.

'Three!'

Crutch whipped the reins, and the horse, already nervy from its burns, reared, then took off, heading straight for the building on the opposite side of the street. The wagon bounced and rocked like a longboat in a storm. The marines were chasing behind the best they could.

'Stop!' yelled a komitav officer from down the street.

Crutch saw the building coming up fast. The horse saw the building and wanted to turn right and run down the main street. Crutch pulled hard on the left rein to get the horse to turn into the side street.

'Stop!' yelled the komitav officer again.

The horse turned to the left just before hitting the building with fear in its eyes. The wagon slid on the cobblestones, slammed into the wall, and kept right on going down the side street.

'Six komitav!' yelled Sergeant Zander behind him. 'Take them at the next corner.'

The horse kept galloping, the wagon rocking and jumping. Crutch pulled back on the reins, and it kept going. He pulled back hard, and the horse skidded to a halt. Crutch softly shook the reins, and the horse started walking. He walked it up to the next corner and around the bend.

Crutch tied the reins of the horse to the railing of a building, then went back to the corner where the marines were concealed, waiting.

'Wait till all six of them come into the street, then start shooting,' whispered Sergeant Zander. 'We don't want any of them getting away and bringing more komitav after us.

The komitav officers came running down the side street fast.

'Where did they go?' said the first officer.

'Came down this street. Must have turned at next street.'

Four komitav officers were in the street now, then five.

When the sixth came around the corner, Longshot shot him in the guts with an arrow. These komitav officers were brave. Instead of running away, they drew their swords and ran straight towards where the arrow came from. Longshot got two more of them before they got to him, one in the face and the other in the chest.

Boulder came out from behind the corner, grabbed the officer at the front by the throat, and smashed his head into the cobblestone street. Sergeant Zander went to stab another with a dagger, but this komitav was quick. He dodged Sergeant Zander's dagger and drew back his sword for a thrust. Crutch stepped from his hiding place and drove the blade on his walking cane into the komitav officer's crotch. As the komitav officer buckled over, Sergeant Zander drove his dagger into the back of his head.

Quicksilver engaged the last standing komitav officer in a sword fight. They were both evenly matched, with their blades ringing against each other as both the komitav officer and Quicksilver looked for an opening. But Quicksilver wouldn't need one.

As the komitav officer turned, Crutch drove the blade on his walking cane through the officers from behind into his heart. Blood spurted from the hole in the komitav officer's back, and he smacked to the cobblestone street as Crutch pulled his blade free.

The first komitav officer Longshot had hit with an arrow crawled on his side towards the main street. Sergeant Zander ran down the side street and cut the komitav officer's throat with his dagger. The officer made gurgling sounds as his blood spilled onto the street.

'Let's pull these bodies up around the corner where no one will see them and get moving,' said Sergeant Zander.

Crutch pulled the closest komitav officer to him around the corner by the arm, being careful not to get blood on himself. He would need clean clothes for later. Boulder dragged in two bodies by the legs, and the other marines dragged one each. They lined the bottom corner of a wall in the shadows with them.

Longshot went and talked to the horse again, stroking its head and giving it words of encouragement.

Before they left, Crutch looked at the komitav officers and said, 'I think we could use these.'

'What do you have in mind?' said Sergeant Zander.

Crutch told the marines his idea, and they spent the next five minutes pulling uniforms off the komitav officers and choosing the best three.

They went through back streets and alleys until they reached the abandoned iron works building. Longshot tied off the horse and gave it more water.

'We'll be back later,' he said as he stroked it.

They closed the huge doors of the building behind them as they left.

'We hide in the sewers until it's time,' said Sergeant Zander.

'Can we hide in the sewers here,' said Longshot. 'It will help keep the horse calm.'

'We can't,' said Sergeant Zander. If someone finds the horse and wagon, the first thing they'll do is a thorough search of the area.'

Longshot nodded.

'Let's get back to where we stashed our gear,' said Sergeant Zander.

Chapter 45
Let Them Burn

They waited in the sewers with their sacks of gear until midnight, then Crutch led the marines through the piss and shit of Teevilgrad to the place where all this began. He peered up through the grate to make sure the street was empty.

'You have enough bluefire for this?' whispered Sergeant Zander.

'We've been in that room at the inn for a month with a bag of rublets and time on our hands,' whispered Quicksilver. 'Did you think we'd just sit around twiddling our thumbs?'

'We might have slipped out a few times to buy some stuff and to set a few things up,' whispered Longshot.

They looked up at the komitav family accommodations. The place where Crutch first met Anton, and Yelena, and their baby Nikolai.

'We already set up bluefire at the base of the building,' whispered Quicksilver. Just need to get it in front of the doors so they can't escape.'

'Do we have to burn this building?' whispered Crutch. 'There could be women and children in there.'

'Anyone who was a true compatriot has taken their families and fled by now,' whispered Sergeant Zander.

'There must still be wives and children in there,' whispered Crutch.

'We can't knock on the doors and tell them to get out while we burn their husbands and fathers,' whispered Sergeant Zander. 'We need to make sure there's no komitav who'll come running or turn up unexpected while we're at the Komitav Operative building getting the glowstone. It's gonna be hard enough as it is.'

'Anyone loyal to Solokov deserves to die,' said Longshot.

'Plus,' whispered Quicksilver. 'Fire!'

'Two minute timers,' said Sergeant Zander. 'One ball of bluefire next to every door.'

Crutch stayed hidden on the street as the other marines slipped silently up the stairs, crouching to stay low, then along the landings, leaving a ball of bluefire next to each door. Quicksilver added some extra bluefire balls near the ones he'd already set to make sure they went off at the same time.

The marines came down the stairs as silently as they went up and got back to Crutch, waiting there in the darkness. Longshot pulled his bow off his back and notched an arrow.

As they waited, Crutch wondered if this would be his life, going from one village or city to the next, setting it on fire. There was Quayside and Honeysap Grove. Now it was Teevilgrad.

One bluefire ball on the top landing sputtered, then burst into flames. A young man came to the door and shouted, 'Fire!' Longshot fired an arrow that went straight through his chest. He dropped to his knees, and the bluefire set him alight.

Then all the bluefire exploded in flames from the base of the building up to the landings. It was a hellstorm of blue flames that quickly turned to yellow and orange flames as the wood in the whole building caught fire.

Crutch could hear the screams of people inside. One man ran out of a door on the ground floor, screaming, his trousers on fire. As he ran to open the next door down, Longshot hit him with an arrow through the back of the head.

Crutch heard men, women, and children screaming for help. The marines stayed where they were, watching and waiting until the screams got softer and they were gone. By then, the building was a burning shell, its roof crumbling in, burning rafters falling through the next floor in a bursting shower of flames and sparks that sprayed across the cobblestone street.

Crutch knew he should feel something for these people, but after Papageenar, he found a way to block out the emotions that came from seeing death. There was a place in him now that was hardened to it. He gave himself some comfort by reminding himself that someone in this building had probably burned the true compatriots hall or done worse.

'Let's get the street urchins and the Brothers of Mercy,' said Sergeant Zander.

Chapter 46

Komitav Accidents

Inside the basement of the run-down building on Sunset Street, the three Brothers of Mercy finished putting on uniforms the marines had pulled off the dead komitav officers.

'Will make safer for you when you do guard job for us and when you escape,' said Crutch.

'Is good idea,' said Torge. He looked closer at the shirt he'd just put on. 'Some blood on this uniform.'

'The officer wearing it had little accident,' said Crutch.

Torge looked even closer at the blood and the slash in the shirt. 'Looks like accident involved sword,' he said.

'I think this one had accident with arrow,' said Martov, looking at the hole in the midriff of his kamitov shirt and sash.

'Mine is good,' said Rohan. 'Except for blood on collar. So much blood.'

'Komitav is dangerous profession,' said Crutch. 'Many accidents. You ready to go?'

'We are ready,' said Torge.

Crutch and Sergeant Zander led the brothers through the sewers all the way to a sewer grate in an alley near the Komitav Operative building. Pavee and around twenty of the older street urchins were waiting there.

'Hello Pavee,' whispered Torge. Pavee smiled and nodded.

'You wait here,' whispered Crutch. 'Boulder will be back in few minutes to get you.'

'Okay,' whispered Pavee. Torge nodded.

Crutch and Sergeant Zander went through the sewers and came to a grate near the abandoned iron works warehouse, where the rest of the marines were waiting for them.

'We go now,' whispered Sergeant Zander.

They went into the warehouse, and Crutch climbed onto the seat of the wagon. The other marines followed behind as Crutch drove the wagon down side streets. After a few minutes, they came to the alley where Crutch had been feeding the komitav officers in the Komitav Operative building late at night.

Crutch parked the wagon next to the door in the usual place, with the rear right next to the door. Sergeant Zander hid underneath the wagon, and the rest of the marines hid on the other side. Crutch knocked on the door, and a komitav officer stuck his head out.

'Crujge,' he said. 'What are you doing here? Is not safe.' Before he said another word, Sergeant Zander rolled out from under the wagon and drove a dagger through his chin up into his head. Crutch stopped the door from closing with his walking cane as Sergeant Zander rolled the komitav officer's body under the wagon.

The marines went through the door and checked the immediate area. No more officers.

'Boulder, get the brothers and the urchins,' whispered Sergeant Zander.

'Yes Sarge.'

'Quicksilver, drag that body up around the corner away from the building so no one sees it.'

'Will do Sarge,' whispered Quicksilver.

Longshot waited at the door while Crutch and Sergeant Zander went into the building.

'If we come across a komitav officer, try to bluff your way through it for now,' whispered Sergeant Zander.

Crutch moved forward, going off his memory of his last time inside the building. He went a couple of corridors away from the vault, then stopped and waited for everyone else to catch up.

Sergeant Zander and the marines came up right next to him.

'Wait here,' said Sergeant Zander to the Brothers of Mercy.

The marines moved silently down the last corridors until they were just outside the vault. Crutch hobbled into view of the two guards on the vault door.

'Compatriots, am lost. Can you tell me where is Anton Ivenko?' Crutch walked into the room to get closer to the guards.

'You can't come in here,' said one guard, drawing his sword.'

'No need for sword, I am old man. Can't fight two strong guards,' said Crutch, then he stepped forward, released the blade on his cane, and drove it into the head of the guard who'd drawn his sword.

The second guard was fast. He had his sword out and swung at Crutch, a sword swing that would have taken Crutch's head off if there wasn't an arrow through the side of his neck.

'Nice shot,' whispered Crutch as the guard fell to the floor.

'Quicksilver, tell the Brothers of Mercy to take up guard positions in the next corridor,' whispered Sergeant Zander. 'We don't want any komitav walking in on us.'

Crutch already had the key to the vault out. The vault door was huge, made of heavy steel. Probably Ironborn steel. Crutch slid the key into the keyhole and tried to turn it. Then he tried to turn it again.

'The key's not working.'

'What?' whispered Sergeant Zander.

'It won't turn.'

'Let me have a try,' whispered Sergeant Zander.

Sergeant Zander jiggled the key, took it out, pushed it back in, tried to turn it, and couldn't get the lock to move.

Torge was walking past the vault to get to the next corridor and stopped. He looked at the two dead bodies, then back up at Sergeant Zander.

'They were being difficult,' whispered Sergeant Zander.

Torge raised his eyebrows. 'Is second tier lock.'

'What?' whispered Sergeant Zander.

'Is second tier lock,' said Torge so softly, it was quieter than a whisper. 'Need to move handle into open position before you can turn key.'

'How do you know this?' whispered Crutch.

'I worked in bank before joining brothers. And don't care about komitav,' said Torge. 'They kill brothers. Happy to kill them all.'

'Your thinking has changed,' said Crutch.

'Is war,' said Torge. 'Brothers of Mercy get name because two hundred years ago they show no mercy to enemies. Name is ironic.'

Crutch opened the handle of the safe door, then Sergeant Zander turned the key. The gears clunked, and the vault door was unlocked.

'Thank you, Torge,' whispered Sergeant Zander. 'Is safer for you and Brothers of Mercy if you don't see what is in vault.'

'Hope what you find in there is worth it. I never find anything good in bank vault.' Torge picked up the two swords from the dead guards and slipped away with Rohan and Mortav to guard the next corridor.

As Sergeant Zander pulled at the door, Crutch could see the orange glow. It swung open, revealing a vault full of glowstone.

'Best thing I've seen all day,' whispered Sergeant Zander. 'Boulder and Quicksilver go in the vault, put the glowstone in the sacks, then bring them out here. We don't want the street urchins to see what they're carrying. The less they know, the better.'

'Yes, Sarge,' whispered Quicksilver.

'I'm a pumpkin,' whispered Boulder.

'Longshot, drag these bodies out and put them somewhere no one will find them. Then manage the loading of the sacks into the barrels on the wagon. Give us a warning if there's any trouble outside.'

'Will do,' said Longshot, grabbing one of the bodies and dragging it to the door, leaving a trail of blood behind him.

Crutch and Sergeant Zander helped throw glowstone into sacks and drag them out into the corridor. Pavee and the street urchins grabbed the sacks and carried them off to the wagon.

'You really think the street urchins won't look inside those sacks?' said Crutch.

'They will look, won't they,' said Sergeant Zander. 'We'll have to tell Pavee that they can never tell anyone what they saw.'

'I'll take care of that, Sarge.'

The loading of the wagon went fast. The vault was half empty in a few minutes. Crutch thought maybe they'd get away without any komitav noticing them.

'Let's join the Brothers of Mercy,' said Sergeant Zander. Boulder and Quicksilver can finish up here.'

Chapter 47
A Talking Mood

When they went out of the vault, Crutch and Sergeant Zander saw the Brothers of Mercy in their komitav uniforms standing in the corridor, watching.

'See anyone?' whispered Sergeant Zander.

'Saw two komitav officers down that junction, but they went past without looking this way,' said Torge.

Then they saw them. At least a dozen fully armed komitav came around the tee junction of corridors, moving straight towards them.

'Think we can bluff through this one, Sarge?' said Crutch.

'They don't look like they're in a talking mood,' said Sergeant Zander.

The corridor was only wide enough for two men to fight shoulder-to-shoulder.

Torge and Rohan moved to the front.

'Remember your training,' said Torge. 'And remember, this is not game.'

'Not game,' said Rohan, 'but I will enjoy.'

The komitav were smart. They had two swordsmen at the front, with two spearmen right behind them. That meant Torge and Rohan would have to fight against four komitav at the same time. Crutch knew from the Kona Track that dodging spear thrusts while someone slashed and thrust at you with a sword was a terrifying experience. And these were komitav. They'd be using their feints and cooperating with each other to make the fight even more dangerous.

Torge immediately evened the odds by deflecting the swing of the komitav swordsman in front of him, jumping on his shoulders, and driving his own sword into the neck of the spearman in the second row, pushing it deep into his body.

Crutch hazarded a guess that the komitav had never trained to fight someone who jumped on their shoulders as a first attack. The komitav officer turned his sword, ready to hack into Torge's legs, but Torge kicked him in the face with his heel. Then Torge jumped back down, keeping hold of the sword in the spearman's body. As it cut down, it went through the komitav swordsman's upper sword arm, cutting it clean off his body.

The arm fell to the floor with the sword. Torge let go of his own sword, still stuck in the spearman who was now falling to the floor with a huge gash from his neck to his chest. Torge fell to one knee, grabbed the sword on the floor, and stabbed up into the komitav officer he'd just cut the arm off. The sword went up through his guts and came out of his back.

On the other side of the corridor, Rohan struggled, dodging spear thrusts while sparring with the komitav swordsman in front of him. Rohan parried and dodged a thrust from the sword, saw his opening, and stepped forward to deliver the killing blow to the swordsman.

Torge yelled, 'No!' but it was too late.

As Rohan came forward, the spear from the spearman in the next row caught him in the guts. Rohan grunted and toppled to the ground on his face as the spearman pulled back his spear. Rohan's blood spilled to the floor.

With one motion, Mortav pulled Rohan's body back by the leg, jumped forward, got Rohan's sword from the floor, and thrust upwards at the komitav swordsman. The sheer speed of the attack caught the komitav officer by surprise, and Mortav drove the sword through his chin and into his head.

Mortav jumped back, missing a thrust for his chest from the spearman who started in the second row, but was now in the front line. A line of spearmen with shields is a deadly thing in battle, but one man with a spear in a corridor against a sword or even a dagger is at a severe disadvantage. Crutch knew Mortav just had to close the distance past the spearhead, and the spear would be useless.

Mortav knew it too. He pushed the spear aside with his sword and moved in for the kill. But the komitav officer was ready for him. As Mortav held his sword up and moved forward, the komitav spearmen let go of his spear with one hand and, at the last second, twisted to avoid the sword thrust, drew a dagger, and stabbed Mortav right through the eye deep into his head.

Crutch was right behind Mortav. This could only work once, if it worked at all. As Mortav fell to the floor, Crutch hunched over, looking as old and feeble as he could. He peered up at the komitav officer and recognised him as someone he'd fed soup to from the wagon before.

'Crujge. What are you...?'

This was no time for sentiment. Crutch brought up his walking cane, released the blade, and thrust it into the komitav officer's chest. The komitav looked at Crutch in shock and surprise. Crutch pulled the blade out and thrust again, this time into the komitav officer's forehead.

As the officer fell, Crutch did a count. Four komitav officers down and eight left. Now Crutch was shoulder-to-shoulder with Torge. These komitav knew how to fight. Crutch knew if they fought hand to hand with them, it was unlikely he'd get out unharmed, if he got out alive.

The komitav officer in front of him came forward. Pretending to be an old, crippled man wouldn't work now. The officer used the full reach of his sword, taking advantage of the fact that Crutch's walking cane was shorter. Crutch parried and dodged, remembering his training, looking for those feints.

He figured his best chance was to get the komitav officer when he came forward in range of Crutch's walking cane. Crutch pretended to slip, hoping the komitav officer would move in for the kill, but the officer just smiled with a slight shake of his head. The officer had seen tricks like that before. He wouldn't be baited.

Crutch moved to his left, then had to dodge to his right and parry with his cane to avoid a sword swing that was just inches from the top of his head. If the fight kept going this way, Crutch knew he'd end up dead.

Quicksilver appeared in the corridor behind him. 'Get back,' he yelled. Crutch saw what Quicksilver had in his hand. Bluefire. He thrust forward with his walking cane, then grabbed Torge by the wrist, turned, and ran back away from the komitav officers. The other marines were already behind him, heading for the safety of the corner.

Quicksilver lobbed one ball of bluefire in a huge throw that landed just behind the komitav officers. They watched it roll behind them and do absolutely nothing.

The next three balls he threw straight at them. The first two fell at their feet, and they smiled and kept coming forward. The third burst into flames right in the leading komitav officer's face. Then the bluefire balls Quicksilver had already thrown burst into blue flames too. The komitav officers were on fire, and they were trapped.

Quicksilver smiled, watching them scream and burn.

'Is the glowstone loaded?' whispered Sergeant Zander.

'Yes, Sarge,' whispered Quicksilver, glancing at Sergeant Zander briefly before turning back to admire his work, the komitav officers crawling on the floor now as fire engulfed their bodies. Flames crept up the walls, and smoke came down the halls as the corridor around the burning komitav officers caught fire.

'Time to go,' whispered Sergeant Zander.

'Do we have to?' whispered Quicksilver. 'The fun is just starting.'

'Come on,' whispered Sergeant Zander, grabbing Quicksilver by the wrist and pulling him away.

They moved as fast as they could, Torge with them. As they passed the room with the vault Crutch looked at the open vault door.

'Wait,' whispered Crutch. 'We should close the vault door. We want to buy as much time as we can before Solokov finds out his glowstone is missing.'

Sergeant Zander ran to the vault door and closed it, while Crutch turned the lock with the key.

Torge came in with them. 'You have dagger?' he said.

Sergeant Zander handed him a dagger, and Torge jammed it into the lock, turned it around, and broke off the blade so the end was stuck in the lock.

'Need to bend handle too,' said Torge.

'Help him, Boulder,' said Sergeant Zander.

Together, Torge and Boulder put their entire weight and strength on the handle of the vault. Crutch could hear the metal bend as smoke drifted to them from the corridor. He could feel the heat of the flames moving fast towards them.

'Is good,' said Torge. Take them hours to open vault now.'

'Thank you, Torge,' said Sergeant Zander. 'Let's get out of here.'

They ran through the corridors with smoke and flames building behind them, then finally out into the alley. The wagon was there, with the street urchins hidden behind the wagon and in the shadows of the alley.

Longshot came out of hiding and took the bridle of the horse. He began leading it to a side street as the street urchins came out of hiding too.

Chapter 48
Leaving Teevilgrad

'So we say goodbye, Torge,' said Crutch. 'Sorry about Rohan and Mortav.'

'Is okay. They died brothers.'

'Maybe some urchins will become brothers.'

'Their choice,' said Torge. 'Your idea is good plan.'

Pavee came over to Crutch, and Crutch gave him half a sack of rublets. 'These are you for you and urchins.'

Pavee looked in the bag, and his eyes went wide. 'All of it?'

'Yes. Did you find land we talked about?'

'Yes. Two of my boys found good spot for sale well out of town.'

'You can take Torge and urchins there through sewers then over country without being seen?'

'Yes. Is easy.'

'Torge will show you how to farm. Remember what we talked about?'

'Yes. We make Volktag drink. Sell to Teevilgrad taverns.'

'Good. And grow food to eat yourself. Torge will teach you.'

Pavee wrapped his arms around Crutch and hugged him. 'Thank you, Crujge. You save my life.'

Crutch's throat was tight. 'You good boy,' said Crutch. 'Make it good life.'

Pavee headed off down the alley with Torge and the street urchins behind him. He pulled up a sewer grate, and the urchins and

Torge climbed down, disappearing like ants. Pavee was the last to go, pulling the grate back down as he went.

Crutch joined the marines and the wagon heading down the side street.

'You should climb up into the seat,' said Sergeant Zander. 'Just in case someone we know sees us.'

'Okay,' said Crutch, climbed on and took the reins.

Behind them, the Komitav Operative building burned bright, black smoke billowing from its roof.

'We still have a long way to go before we get to the docks at Kodil Bay,' said Sergeant Zander. 'Let's pick up the pace. And keep up your guard.'

The marines started jogging. Crutch felt guilty that he was sitting in the wagon, but was glad for the rest. They stuck to the side streets and alleys, heading for the city gates that led out to Kodil Bay. They were making good progress and half way down a side street when they saw a group of komitav officers crossing three intersections down behind them.

'Run and turn at the next corner,' whispered Sergeant Zander. 'Maybe they won't see us.'

As soon as they started running, the wagon made a grinding, squeaking sound then one of the back wheels fell off.

'Dammit!' said Sergeant Zander.

Crutch heard the komitav officers yelling and saw at least a dozen were now running towards them.

'Can you and Quicksilver lead them away, then circle back?' said Sergeant Zander.

'We can do that, Sarge,' said Longshot.

'Once they're gone, we'll get the wagon fixed and head for the last side street before the city gates to Kodil Bay.'

'We'll meet you there, Sarge.'

Crutch, Boulder, and Sergeant Zander hid in the shadows of the buildings on the street as Longshot and Quicksilver ran back towards the komitav officers, then turned down the first intersection. Most of the komitav officers turned and chased after them when they got to the corner, but two kept walking towards the wagon.

'Waste of time running around, chasing after wagon in middle of night,' said the first komitav officer as they came up to the broken wheel.

'Never know. Might be rebels or those filthy true compatriots,' said the second komitav officer.

'You look for me?' said Crutch, stepping out of the shadows.

The second komitav officer looked up in surprise and drew his sword. 'Is Crujge. We get fifty gold rublets for catching him.'

'Is good night,' said the first officer, pulling his sword.

The second officer moved closer to Crutch. 'You come with us, Crujge,' He put out his arm to grab Crutch, and Sergeant Zander's face and knife arm appeared out of the darkness behind him. Sergeant Zander cut his throat, and the komitav officer dropped to the ground.

Boulder was behind the first komitav officer. He grabbed the officer's head and wrenched it around hard. Crutch could hear the neck snap and watched his body fall to the ground. Boulder and Sergeant Zander dragged the bodies around the corner and out of sight.

Crutch was looking at the wheel when Sergeant Zander and Boulder came back. Sergeant Zander knelt down and looked at the axle underneath the wagon.

'The axle's alright. It's just the flange that's got bent and come off. We can get this back on and fix it. Let's hope we don't get any more visitors while we're doing it.'

'What do you need?' whispered Crutch.

'Just some manpower,' whispered Sergeant Zander, fiddling with the outside hub of the wheel. 'Can you lift this side of wagon, Boulder?'

'Yes, Sarge.'

Boulder lifted the wagon up, and Sergeant Zander got Crutch to help him guide the wheel back onto the axle. Sergeant Zander used a rock to get the flange back onto the hub of the wheel, securing the axle.

'That should do it,' whispered Sergeant Zander, 'but it's a rough fix.'

'Will it hold?' whispered Crutch.

'It should, but I don't know how well. We'll have to take it slow.'

They took off again, this time at a steady walking pace. Crutch went on foot to keep the weight in the wagon down.

'This has to be the slowest getaway we've ever done,' whispered Sergeant Zander.

'That's true,' whispered Crutch.

'Remember that time in Warmhaven when you saved us from the Estovians with that farmer's wagon?'

'I'd hoped you'd forgotten,' whispered Crutch.

'Came down that hill at a full gallop, whipping the reins, and you didn't even know how to drive,' whispered Sergeant Zander, then laughed.

'You brought us a cart,' whispered Boulder, smiling. 'But no soup.'

'Sorry Boulder.'

'It's okay,' whispered Boulder. 'In Teevilgrad, you brought everyone soup.'

'Your turning has improved since then,' whispered Sergeant Zander, then broke out laughing again.

They made the last side street before the city gates and waited. Crutch looked back the way they'd come.

'Some fire back there,' he whispered.

'Looks like Quicksilver and Longshot have been busy,' whispered Sergeant Zander.

He'd barely mentioned their names when they came running around the corner.

'Was all that fire I can see over there your doing?' whispered Sergeant Zander.

'Could've been,' whispered Quicksilver.

'Good work,' whispered Sergeant Zander.

'Yes, it was definitely us,' whispered Quicksilver, smiling.

They left the wagon in the side street and crept to the corner. Up ahead, Crutch could see the gates that led out to Kodil Bay. They were closed and guarded.

'I might be able to talk us through,' whispered Crutch.

'You could try,' whispered Quicksilver. 'But me and Longshot planned for this.

Crutch tried to imagine what the plan would be like if Quicksilver made it. He didn't have to wait long to find out.

Longshot pulled out an arrow with some kind of black goo near the head. Quicksilver lit it, and Longshot fired at the base of the city gates on the left. They exploded into an inferno of blue fire. Longshot pulled another arrow from his quiver and Quicksilver lit that one too. Longshot fired to the base of the city gates on the right. Those exploded into blue flame too.

The gates burned hot. Half a dozen guards ran away from the fire, standing in front of the burning gate, weapons drawn, ready to fight whoever was firing at them from the darkness.

'So predictable,' said Longshot as he notched another arrow, and Quicksilver lit it. He shot straight at the guards' feet, and blue fire shot up from the ground, setting four of the guards on fire. The other two fled into the darkness as their compatriots fell to the ground in flames, screaming.

'How did you get bluefire at the base of the city gates?' said Sergeant Zander.

'Amazing what street urchins will do for a gold rublet,' said Quicksilver.

'You had street urchins running around carrying balls of bluefire?' said Crutch.

'Can't have all the fun myself,' said Quicksilver. 'I have to think about the next generation.'

'You are one crazy bastard,' said Sergeant Zander.

The burning gates swung open and collapsed to the ground.

'After you,' said Quicksilver, proudly ushering the marines forward as if he were guiding them through the entrance to a ball.

Chapter 49

The Long Road To Kodil Bay

Once they got the wagon past the light of the burning gates, Quicksilver went ahead with a torch to make sure they stayed on the road. Longshot walked with the horse holding its bridle, while Sergeant Zander, Boulder, and Crutch walked alongside the wagon.

'I don't know how much longer this horse is gonna last,' said Longshot. 'If we push him too long, he can die.'

'We'll all be dead if we don't get to Kodil Bay before word gets there of the rebellion in Teevilgrad and Solokov's new "enemy of the people",' said Sergeant Zander.

Longshot nodded.

They walked into the night along the road, listening to the axle creak, hoping it didn't fall off again, checking behind them constantly, worried that a messenger would come running out of the night for Teevilgrad or that someone was chasing them.

'Do you think Solokov knows we're headed this way?' said Crutch.

'Those guards at the gate saw us and ran,' said Sergeant Zander. 'We can hope they didn't tell anyone, but hope can get you killed. Better to assume the worst.'

They were walking for three hours at their slow pace when the horse stopped. Its breathing was heavy and laboured, its coat was lathered in sweat, and its hind legs were trembling.

Longshot held the bridle, stroked the horse's head, and tried to lead it forward. It wouldn't move. Not a step.

'This horse doesn't have anything left in him,' said Longshot.

'Untether it,' said Sergeant Zander. 'We'll have to push the wagon by hand. Are you up to taking the front Boulder?'

'I can do it, Sergeant Zander.'

'Good man.'

Longshot untethered the horse, talking to it the whole time. 'Good boy. You've done a good job.'

Once the horse was free of the weight of the wagon, it walked forward on unsteady legs to the side of the road where it stood, wheezing. Longshot took off its reins and gave it a drink of water from his waterskin.

'You'll be alright, boy. Catch your breath and eat some of this grass at the side of the road.'

'Time to go,' said Sergeant Zander.

'With you,' said Longshot, going to the back of the wagon with Crutch and Sergeant Zander.

Quicksilver set his torch in the front of the wagon near the seat so they could see where they were going, then joined them at the back.

Boulder lifted the front of the wagon, and Sergeant Zander called, 'Push.'

Crutch pushed off with his good leg, and the wagon started moving slowly. The road was on a slight slope downhill, which made the pushing easier. They went for fifteen minutes down the road that way when Crutch looked behind them.

Way off in the distance, he could see torches. He looked back again a minute later, and while they were still way off, the torches were getting closer.

'There's someone behind us,' said Crutch as he pushed.

Sergeant Zander looked back for a few seconds. 'Looks like the komitav are chasing us,' he said. 'We need to go faster.' Sergeant Zander started calling out a rhythm for steps: 'One, two, one, two.' It was a steady pace. Much faster, but not so fast they'd be exhausted within a few minutes.

Crutch only pushed with his good leg on the count of one. He could hear Boulder's heavy breathing at the front of the wagon. The last horse had nearly collapsed from pulling the wagon. He wondered how long Boulder could do it.

Crutch looked back and saw the torches were getting closer. He thought he could make out red sashes.

'They're gaining on us. Looks like komitav.'

'Solokov's last little gift for us,' said Sergeant Zander. 'Can you go faster, Boulder?'

'Yes, Sarge,' said Boulder in between gasps of breath.

'You sure?' said Sergeant Zander.

'I'm sure,' said Boulder, then took in another huge breath.

Sergeant Zander picked up his cadence. Now they were close to a slow jog. The hill got just a little steeper going down, which helped.

A few minutes later, Crutch looked back, and they were closer. Much closer. In the light of their torches, he could clearly see black uniforms and red sashes.

'It's komitav,' said Crutch. 'They're running now.'

They came over a bump in the road, and the docks were in view at the bottom of a long hill. Maybe they could make it.

'Full speed,' yelled Sergeant Zander.

Crutch had no idea where Boulder found the strength or the energy, but he started sprinting, holding the wagon up with his arms. With his good leg, Crutch gave it everything he had. He could hear Sergeant Zander, Quicksilver, and Longshot gasping for air as they sprinted to keep up, pushing as hard as they could.

The wagon bounced on every rock and every tiny divot. Behind them, Crutch could hear shouting.

'Don't let them get away!'

Crutch recognised the voice. Arch Warden Gragor.

The sun broke over the bay; it's first light streaming across the water and up the road. Crutch saw guards coming out of the watch house near the docks. Four of them. They could deal with four guards.

Then ten more came out, fully armed. Behind the wagon, he saw Arch Warden Gragor and his five wardens, with a dozen komitav officers behind them.

'Stop Boulder,' said Sergeant Zander. 'Catch your breath. We'll have to fight.'

Boulder set down the wagon, wheezing and gasping for breath.

Gragor's men were close now. Crutch could see many of the komitav were wounded. Two had bandaged arms, one had a bandage around his midriff, and two more had half their faces bandaged. Clearly, it had been a bad night for Solokov's men.

The guards from the Kodil Bay watch house were getting closer too. Behind them, out in the bay, Crutch could see the Auld Faithful. The crew there were lowering longboats and piling on board with weapons. But they were too far away.

Crutch and the marines were outnumbered, poorly armed, and the crew of the Auld Faithful would take too long to get to them. Crutch turned back to the komitav.

'Crujge,' said Gragor. 'You nearly escape. So close, but no one escapes Arch Warden Gragor.'

'Not escaping,' said Crutch, pulling his walking cane from his belt and hunching over like an old man. 'Just leaving Teevilgrad. Ship is just finishing quarantine. Good time to leave.'

'You think we are fools?' said Gragor. 'What is in wagon?'

'Just arts and crafts from street urchins of Teevilgrad,' said Crutch. Very popular with rich nobles in Uraskova.'

'Story is so bad I don't even have to check barrels,' said Gragor.

'Is shame,' said Crutch. 'Might really like one of toy horses made from hardened dog turd.'

'What?'

'Dog turd craft suit you perfect,' said Crutch. 'Match your face.'

If Crutch died tonight, he'd at least get the satisfaction of putting this arsehole Gragor in his place.

Chapter 50
Victory For All

'You think you funny? You are enemy of magnificent Emperor Igor Solokov and enemy of people. Like other filthy true compatriots, I enjoy watching you die. Shoot him officer,' said Arch Warden Gragor.

The officer with a bandaged face holding a crossbow did nothing.

'Shoot him!' yelled Gragor.

The kamitov officer raised his crossbow at Crutch, then fired a crossbow bolt straight through the back of Gragor's head. Crutch saw the bolt come out of Gragor's face as his body jerked and dropped to the ground. The kamitov officer dropped his crossbow, drew his sword, and cut down another warden before the warden had a chance to realise what was going on.

Boulder jumped towards one warden. The warden moved to his right, just like Boulder expected from the practice they'd done to fight komitav officers. Boulder used his movement against him, slamming into his side hard so the warden smashed into another warden beside him. Boulder caught the warden's wrist as he fell, broke it, and snatched the sword in his hand away.

Boulder thrust the sword straight through the other warden's chest, then finished off the warden he'd already injured by stabbing him through the throat.

Sergeant Zander dodged a sword from another warden, or at least he pretended to dodge it. They'd trained against the komitav strategies so much by now that the first feint attack was totally predictable to them.

Sergeant Zander pretended to dodge the first feint, then dodged the real attack, brought up his dagger, and shoved it straight into the side of the warden's neck. Then he jumped back out of range, just in case the attack didn't kill the warden.

The warden's eyes glazed over, and he crumpled, blood from his neck staining the dirt of the road.

Quicksilver engaged in another protracted sword fight with a warden. They made an impressive array of feints and thrusts, parries, and dodges. Longshot drew his bow and shot the warden Quicksilver was fighting in the back with an arrow. As he fell, Quicksilver cut his head clean off.

Another warden came for Crutch with his sword.

Crutch heard the bandaged komitav yell, 'No!' as the warden swung at Crutch. This warden thought he was cutting down a helpless old man. Crutch ducked the sword swing, sprung the blade on his walking cane, and drove it straight through he warden's throat.

'Good riddance,' said Crutch as the warden dropped to the ground. 'Should never try to hurt helpless old man.'

'Komitav, lay down arms!' yelled the komitav with bandages on his face. These are friends.' The ten komitav officers stood down.

'Uncle, are you okay?'

'Is that you, Anton?' said Crutch. Best to hide the fact that he knew who it was before he baited Gragor.

The komitav officer took the bandages off his face. 'Is me.' The komitav officer next to Anton took the bandages off his face too. Anton's friend Yevgeny.

'So glad to see you, Anton,' said Crutch. 'Am okay. For now.' Crutch turned and looked at the watch house guards coming towards them fully armed.'

'I am Anton Ivenko from the Teevilgrad komitav,' yelled Anton. 'There has been rebellion in city. Men we killed were komitav rebels. They try to steal this honest merchant's cargo.'

Inside, Crutch laughed to himself. He wasn't the only one who could spin a good story.

Crutch saw the crew of the Auld Faithful and caught the eye of Cedric coming up the docks. While Anton was distracted talking to the guards, Crutch put his finger to his lips. Cedric nodded and passed the message on to the rest of the crew. Silence. Don't talk.

A guard at the back spoke. 'Is true. I know Anton Ivenko. He runs true compatriots soup kitchen, where they give away soup free. My ma and pa go there. I went last time I was in Teevilgrad.'

'And this merchant?' said the captain of the guards.

'He is Crujge. He is merchant who gives money to run soup kitchen. Is good man.'

In a stroke of luck, news musn't have made it to Kodil Bay that the true compatriots and the soup kitchen were now 'enemies of the people.'

The captain of the guard looked at them for a few seconds. 'So we see end of some rebels and saved good man. Is good day.'

'Is good day,' said Anton, smiling.

The captain of the guard turned and saw the crew of the Auld Faithful on the docks. 'These men are under quarantine. Should not be off ship!'

'Forgive them, captain,' said Crutch. 'Quarantine is over in two days, and you can see they don't have death grip. We leave now anyway.'

'You leave now?'

'Yes.'

'Okay. Tell your crew stay away from my guards.'

'I will,' said Crutch. Crutch looked at Anton. 'Could you help push wagon to docks?'

Anton smiled. 'Of course.'

Boulder got at the front of the wagon and picked up the wooden struts. Anton, his friend Yevgeny, and the marines pushed the wagon down to the docks, where the crew of the Auld Faithful started loading the barrels of glowstone onto the longboats.

'Be careful,' whispered Crutch, taking Cedric to one side. 'There's crocs in the water.'

'Not so many now,' whispered Cedric. 'We ran out of pigs, and we've been eating croc meat the last two weeks.'

Crutch laughed. He went back to Anton and took him aside. 'Where is Yelena?'

'Yelena and Nikolai are safe,' said Anton. 'I heard about Solokov searching out true compatriots just in time from friends in komitav. Most of them got away to safe place.'

'I am happy,' said Crutch.

'Some didn't,' said Anton.

'I know,' said Crutch. 'I saw hangings in People's Plaza.'

'Was wrong,' said Anton. 'Solokov must pay.'

'What happened at palace?' said Crutch. 'I see many people with spears and knives head that way.'

'Thousands of angry people go to palace gates. But Solokov called out army. Army would not kill innocent civilians but would not let them through gates either.'

'So what happened?'

'Don't know. I told you all I heard. I was hiding with Yelena and other true compatriots when friend from komitav came and told me Arch Warden Gragor was rounding up komitav officers at palace to chase you to Kodil Bay. Me and Yevgeny disguise ourselves, bring all good komitav we know with us, and follow them.'

'So glad you did,' said Crutch.

'We walk for hours,' said Anton. 'Pass horse on side of road. Gragor said you couldn't get far without horse.'

'Horse was exhausted, said Crutch. 'We set him free.'

Anton nodded. 'When we get closer, I see you hold torch on seat of wagon while Boulder pulled from front. Was amazing show of strength, Boulder.'

'I'm a pumpkin,' said Boulder, smiling as he walked past carrying one of the barrels by himself.

So Anton couldn't see from behind that Crutch pushed the wagon too. Sometimes you see what you want to see, especially when it's dark.

'Thought you might get away, but Gragor made us run. Really wanted you dead,' said Anton. 'He was very bad man.'

The crew knocked the lid of one of the barrels off as they lugged it into the longboat. From where he stood, Crutch could see the sack inside, with the orange glow coming through the fabric. Crutch fetched the barrel lid out of the water with his hand and passed it back to the crew, who put it back on the barrel.

'Careful with cargo,' said Crutch. 'Is all I have left in world.'

If Anton noticed the orange glow, he didn't say anything.

'Where you go now, uncle?' said Anton. 'Can't go back to Uraskova. Nowhere is safe for you now in Estovia.'

Crutch waved Anton in so he could whisper.

'Is okay. I go to Ironbay.'

'Ironbay?' whispered Anton, surprised.

'I trade with Ironbay for years before war. I have friend in high place in navy.'

'Really?' whispered Anton.

'Yes. I will be safe there.' The irony of that statement wasn't lost on Crutch. With someone in Ironbay trying to kill them, he was definitely not safe there. Still, it was a great improvement on being a covert agent in Teevilgrad.

'I will miss you, uncle.'

'I miss you too, nephew. You, and Yelena, and Nikolai can come with me if you want.'

'Thank you, uncle, but I still love Teevilgrad. Is my home.'

'I understand,' whispered Crutch. And he did. He'd seen more love in the true compatriots of Teevilgrad than he thought was possible. 'If you ever get captured by Ironborn or end up in Ironbay, tell them Office 451.'

'Office 451?'

'Yes. Is important you remember this. Say Office 451 and my name. Have friend in high place in navy office. Will save your life.'

'Thank you, uncle. I will remember. Sorry soup kitchen didn't work out.'

'So am I, but was really something for a while.'

'Yes, it was.'

'You are good man, Anton. Teevilgrad needs you. Keep fighting to make Estovia better for all Estovians.'

'Thank you, uncle. I will.' Anton pulled Crutch into a hug.

'Victory for all,' said Crutch.

'Victory for all.'

Boulder and Sergeant Zander helped Crutch onto the longboat, and they pushed off.

Crutch looked back at Anton there on the docks. Anton saluted him, and Crutch saluted right back.

Chapter 51
Burn And Be Proud

As the longboats got close to the Auld Faithful, Cedric whispered, 'That may be the most remarkable thing I've seen, and I've seen a lot. That man thought you were his uncle.'

'He did,' whispered Crutch.

'You saved us having to battle those guards,' said one of the crew.

'You're a bloody legend, Crutch.'

'Your blood's worth bottling.'

'Okay men,' whispered Cedric. 'We're not out of Estovia yet. We can congratulate Crutch later.'

The crew were happy to be leaving. Cedric had ordered them to talk in a whisper, even when they were below deck. Over a month whispering to each other was driving them crazy. Once the Auld Faithful was away from Kodil Bay, Cedric told them they could talk softly below deck, but they should keep the talk to a whisper on deck.

They were still in Estovian waters, and there was a long way to sail before they were safe. They didn't want to get this far, then have some Estovian fisherman bring down a warship on them.

Cedric and the marines were in the galley.

'It won't take long before word gets to Kodil Bay that he let the 'enemy of the people' go,' said Sergeant Zander.

'Do you think Solokov will send warships after us?' said Cedric.

'If he has the warships to send, he will,' said Sergeant Zander. 'Teevilgrad was in open rebellion when we left.'

'It'll only take one warship, and we're sunk,' said Crutch. 'We don't have any ballistas to defend ourselves.'

'Then we'll have to think of other ways to do it,' said Sergeant Zander. 'We're marines. We always find a way.'

'Not me,' said Boulder. 'I'm a pumpkin.'

Cedric and the marines burst out laughing.

They sailed until they were only an hour from leaving Estovian waters. Just when Crutch thought they may have pulled this mission off, the lookout blew his whistle four times. The warning signal for an enemy ship.

It was on them fast. Too fast. An Estovian navy warship with a line of ballistas down each side. And it was quicker than the Auld Faithful.

Crutch scanned the water for a reef or some rocks. Anything they could use to help them get away. There was nothing.

The ship came alongside them, its crew manning a row of ballistas on the deck of the warship, ready to fire.

'No one has to die,' yelled a voice from the warship. 'But if you fight, we kill you all.'

Cedric gave the signal for the crew to put down their weapons as the Estovian crew threw grappling hooks over the rail of the Auld Faithful.

Crutch cursed their bad luck. They'd survived six weeks in the heart of Teevilgrad, shoulder to shoulder with the Komitav. They got into Komitav's most heavily guarded building and stole their most valuable asset. And they got away from Teevilgrad clean, only for a random Estovian warship to capture them just ten miles inside Estovian territorial waters. Another hour, and they would have been free.

'Prepare to be boarded,' said the voice from the Estovian Warship.

Crutch stood at the rail. Somehow, he had to try to talk their way out of this one.

Then the captain of the Estovian warship appeared and walked over the rails to get on board the Auld Faithful.

'Crujge. I thought I recognise ship,' said Inspector Petrov.

'Inspector Petrov,' said Crutch, smiling. 'You have ship upgrade.'

'Is Captain Petrov now. I change career.'

'But you were so good as border patrol officer.'

'Is good for while, but Emperor Solokov not happy with tariffs I bring in. Thinks I stop food getting to nobles. Not happy.'

'Where did he get this idea?' said Crutch smiling.

'I don't know. Is mystery. Anyway, time to spread my wings. Try a little freelancing.'

'Piracy?' said Crutch.

'I work for Estovian government whole life. Titles are important. I like to call myself 'wealth redistribution officer."

'Where did you get Estovian warship?'

'Funny thing. Navy crews in Teevilgrad unhappy with Emperor Solokov. Say things like, 'We burn so Solokov can stay fat and safe in palace with golden poodles.' My favourite is something crew says often. 'Be proud and burn.' Don't know where they get this from, but some say old man in tavern with walking stick tell them all about what is really happening in war. Tell them they should die gloriously and be proud they die for magnificent Emperor Solokov. You know about this Crujge?'

'I am simple merchant,' said Crutch. 'I know nothing of navy or war.'

'Yes, simple merchant,' said Petrov, smiling. 'Anyway, navy men unhappy need new captain. I need career alternative to spending rest of short life in Teevilgrad komitav prison. Is perfect match.'

'Good to see you safe,' said Crutch. 'I am very happy.'

'Good to see you safe too,' said Petrov. 'Before I leave Teevilgrad, street urchins nowhere to be found. Maybe you know what happen to them?'

'I heard they left city to take up careers in agriculture. Is good industry.'

Petrov laughed. 'You are good man, clever man. I knew you would have plan to keep street urchins safe.'

'Not me,' said Crutch, smiling. 'I am just simple merchant.' Crujge dug in his pocket and thought about how much money he had left on him. Just a few rublets. 'How much you want Petrov?'

'Crujge, I am insulted. Your rublets are no good with me. We are brothers. Street urchins from the sewers.'

'You make terrible pirate,' said Crutch.

'Am just starting,' said Petrov.

'Pirate crew will be unhappy you didn't rob us,' said Crutch. 'They want plunder.' He looked at Petrov's crew of border patrol crew, navy recruits, and staid navy officers. They were about as far from a pirate crew as you could imagine.

'Sounds like you know about life of wealth redistribution,' said Petrov. 'You have tips?'

Crutch thought about Captain Wyld and his time as part of that pirate crew.

'I don't know much. Just what I hear from others. Maybe stay away from Skull Cove and never get on jamaroot.' Then a picture of Honeysap Grove in flames and the warehouse falling into a heap of burned timbers flashed through his mind. 'And never drink honeysap rum.'

'Is strange advice, but I think you know more about this than you pretend. I will take advice,' said Petrov.

'Thank you for helping with soup kitchen,' said Crutch.

'Was best thing I ever do in my life. For small time, I think maybe we change Teevilgrad. Make it better.'

'I did too,' said Crutch.

'Was beautiful dream,' said Petrov.

Petrov shook Crutch's hand. A little of the brown face paint Crutch used on his skin to make it look old had run from getting soaked in the sea water and rubbed on the barrel lid as they loaded on Kodil Bay. It rubbed off on Petrov's hand as they shook. Petrov looked down at it, wiped the face paint off on his pants, and looked back up at Crutch.

'Goodbye, friend,' said Petrov. 'I hope we meet again.'

'So do I,' said Crutch.

Petrov turned, stepped up onto the rail, and over onto the Estovian warship. His crew freed the grappling hooks, and the ship pulled away.

Chapter 52
The Greatest Mission

Once they were a day's sailing out of Estovian waters, Cedric relaxed and gave the order that everyone could speak normally again. A cheer went up from the crew. That night, they celebrated in the galley with an extra ration of rum. Crutch was thrilled to finally take off the face paint and the disguise. He'd had enough of hobbling around looking like an old man.

'Explain to me what you did in Teevilgrad,' said Cedric.

'Crutch set up a soup kitchen,' said Sergeant Zander.

'We started by feeding the street urchins,' said Crutch.

'I liked the street urchins,' said Boulder. 'They were my friends.'

'So they played with you?' said Cedric.

'Yes. They didn't care that I was a pumpkin.'

Cedric and the marines laughed.

'The street urchins loved Boulder,' said Crutch. 'They'd climb all over him like he was a huge statue.'

'I still don't understand how a soup kitchen feeding the street urchins of Teevilgrad helped your mission.'

'It started with the street urchins, but Crutch here is not just a master of disguise,' said Sergeant Zander. 'He's a master of logistics. I've never seen anything like it. In no time, we were feeding over ten thousand people.'

'How?' said Cedric.

'I used what you taught me about logistics on a ship,' said Crutch. 'Inspector Petrov helped us buy food from the docks that was meant for the nobles of Teevilgrad. Best of all, the people of Teevilgrad all pulled together and donated what they had. People started growing greens and catching crocodile.'

'It was a beautiful thing,' said Sergeant Zander. 'It got so huge, Solokov could see he was losing control of the city. He tried to stop it.'

'He tried to stop you feeding starving people?'

'Exactly. He hanged women and children who were workers in the soup kitchen in their public square.'

'That must have gone down well,' said Cedric.

'Led to full-on rebellion,' said Sergeant Zander.

'A friend helped us get the key to the vault, and we used the chaos of the rebellion to get the glowstone and get it out of Teevilgrad.'

'You left out all the fires I set,' said Quicksilver.

'We left out a lot of stuff,' said Sergeant Zander.

'But the fires were the best part,' said Quicksilver.

'Who was the man from Teevilgrad who saved you on the docks?' said Cedric.

'That was Anton. He was the leader of the true compatriots, the people we started the soup kitchen with.'

'And he thought you were his uncle?'

'Yes.'

'Amazing.'

'Anton is an amazing man,' said Crutch. 'Solokov must see him as a real threat now.'

'It wasn't just food,' said Sergeant Zander. 'The true compatriots were building a movement. People who wanted change.'

'If Anton was the ruler of Estovia, we wouldn't be at war with them,' said Crutch. 'That's for certain.'

'Well, that's something we can hope for,' said Cedric.

'If he survives,' said Sergeant Zander. 'Solokov will be hunting him now.'

'You should all be proud,' said Cedric. 'You've achieved the impossible getting the glowstone out of Teevilgrad. And you've struck a blow to Solokov that we can only hope will be the end of him.'

Crutch and the marines all thanked Cedric, but Crutch didn't feel proud. He thought of the burning wreckage they'd left behind in

Teevilgrad. Huge parts of their city were on fire. The people were in armed rebellion. Solokov had mobilised the army to protect the palace against innocent civilians. The navy was in disarray. They didn't have the young men they needed to plant and harvest crops in Uraskova.

He should be celebrating that Ironbay's greatest enemy was now weak and ready for a final blow. But now that he knew the people of Teevilgrad, he took no joy in it. He felt deep sadness for good people oppressed by a tyrant and corrupt officials who took advantage of them in every way.

'A toast,' said Cedric, his deep voice booming through the galley. 'To the marines of the Auld Faithful who just successfully completed the greatest mission by a marine squad in the history of Ironbay.'

The crew cheered and drank and cheered and drank and drank again.

Chapter 53

You'll Like Grandma

Spirits in the crew were high when they sailed into the harbour of Ironbay. Most thought they might never see Ironbay again, and here they were pulling into the docks.

Within an hour, family members got word and started turning up to the Auld Faithful, waiting to see their husbands, their fathers, and their sons. There were happy hugs, joyous laughter, and relieved tears. There was everything you'd expect from a homecoming for a ship sent to war.

Everything except Abagail.

Crutch stood at the rail of the Auld Faithful, hoping he'd see Abagail with her wonderful, crooked face running down the docks, but she never came. As the sun began to set, he realised he would have to face the fact that he'd lost her forever. There was a hole in Crutch's heart that nothing but Abagail could fill. He longed to see those ocean blue eyes, see that smile. Just a glimpse would be enough to keep his spirit alive. But there'd be no glimpse, no happy laughter for him, no relieved tears.

'Come have dinner with me and grandma,' said Boulder.

'Thank you, Boulder, but I can't.'

'Why not?'

'I can't just turn up at your grandma's for dinner,' said Boulder. 'She won't be expecting me.'

'Grandma says I can always bring my friends to dinner.'

Crutch worried that Abagail might come and he'd miss her, but he knew he was just kidding himself. If she hadn't come by now, she wouldn't be coming.

He just had to accept that it was over between him and Abagail. He was a commoner, and she was the daughter of an admiral. It was never going to work.

'Okay Boulder. I'd love to come.'

'Good,' said Boulder. 'You'll like grandma. She gives you cake.'

Boulder and Crutch walked through the streets of Ironbay, down King's Way, and then into the side streets until Boulder led them to a little cottage that was part of a row of cottages. Crutch recognised them. Widow's cottages for the army.

When he was a street urchin, the women here would give you food, but they rarely had much to spare. Grief had driven some of the women crazy, and they'd shriek at you or burst out sobbing and wailing. Army guards patrolled here too, and they'd give you a kicking if they found you hanging around the cottages.

Boulder knocked, and his grandma opened the door. Her face filled with delight when she saw Boulder.

Boulder grinned. 'Hi grandma.'

His grandma threw her arms around him. 'I was so happy when I heard you'd made it back safe, Boulder. And who is this young man?'

'This is Crutch.'

'Crutch! Boulder talks about you all the time.' Grandma gave Crutch a huge hug.

'Crutch is my friend.'

'Yes Boulder. You told me how he saved your life more than once. I appreciate you looking after my grandson,' said Grandma. 'You both come inside now. Your timing is perfect. Dinner is ready.'

Crutch sat and ate with Boulder and his grandma. Boulder told her about how he was a pumpkin and Crutch was an old man, and there were street urchins in Teevilgrad, and they were his friends, and they had a big soup kitchen, and Inspector Petrov gave them sugar plums, and the horse got worn out so Boulder had to be the horse, and had to run really fast, and his legs really hurt.

Grandma listened to every word Boulder said. Her eyes glowed with affection for him, even if what Boulder said couldn't possibly have made any sense to her.

Then Boulder said, 'And Crutch lost his girlfriend Abagail.'

Grandma looked at Crutch. 'I'm so sorry to hear that. I remember the day I lost my Fredrick. I always try to remember the happy memories. Never dwell on the way he... the way he went. Do you have happy memories of Abagail?'

Crutch thought of that first time he met her. She said he looked dashing in his new dress uniform and invited Crutch to her birthday party. He remembered that she laughed at him eating, and they danced. He could see her now, racing out onto the landing of the Admiral's residence, jumping into his arms after they broke the Siege of Ironbay.

He remembered her standing on the docks waiting for her when he came back from Papageenar and standing there with Corporal Travis and Tilly's baby. And he remembered them in the longboat in the harbour of Ironbay, her arm around him, both of them looking up at the stars.

'Yes,' said Crutch, trying not to let his voice break.

'You hang on tight to those. My Fredrick died in the first war with Estovia. After the Siege of Crestona and the truce, we were never supposed to fight with them again. And here's you boys back in another war with them.

'How did you lose your Abagail?'

'Abagail is the daughter of the admiral. She's born to nobility, and I'm a commoner. I don't fit in with the kind of boy they want their daughter to be with.'

Boulder's grandma looked at him and sighed. 'Life is a funny thing. When you're young, you're too busy thinking of the future. You don't think much of the past. But when you're older, you don't have many years to look forward to. The past is all you really have, and you start to ponder the choices you made and the paths you went down.

'I don't know Abagail, and I don't know the nobles and how they live. One thing I understand is regrets. You'll regret a few of the things you did in your life, but more than anything, you'll regret the words you never said and the things you didn't do.

'Looking back on my life, not for a second did I regret marrying Fredrick. They all told me he was a wild army brute, and he'd never make a good husband. But with me, he was sweet and kind as Boulder here, and we were happy. We were so happy.'

Grandma sat there looking into space with a wistful look on her face, lost in some memory of the past, a lover she could only touch in her mind.

Eventually, she came back to them. She looked at Crutch and said, 'You can live on the memories you have, but life is about living, so you make new memories you'll never want to forget. I hope you see your Abagail again, but if you don't, someone else will come along.'

Crutch felt a pain deep in his gut. Just the thought of any girl except Abagail left his brain reeling. He simply couldn't imagine it.

'Now would you like some cake?' said Grandma.

'Yes, please,' said Boulder. 'I like cake.'

Crutch's instincts as a street urchin overcame any pain he felt over Abagail. 'I'd love some cake, grandma.'

Chapter 54
I Can't Survive Without Abagail

Late the next day, a young female housemaid came to the Auld Faithful. Crutch immediately recognised her as the young woman who'd served their table at the Admiral's residence and run out of the dining room crying.

Crutch walked down the gangplank to meet her on the docks.

'Corporal Crutch, I'm so glad you're here and you're okay.'

'How can I help you?' said Crutch.

'I'm Jenny, the housemaid at Admiral Hastings.'

'I remember,' said Crutch.

'It's Abagail,' said Jenny. 'She missed you terribly when you were away.'

'She did?'

'Yes. They wouldn't let her leave the house to come see you off. It wasn't right. And now they won't let her leave the house to come see you.'

'When she didn't come, I thought she didn't want to see me any more,' said Crutch.

Jenny looked visibly upset when Crutch said that.

'Abagail and I have been close friends for years. She loves you more than ever. She cries herself to sleep worrying about you. All she wants is to see you again, but they won't let her out. It's not right. It's just not right.'

Crutch went up the steps to the Admiral's residence. Corporal Levi was guarding the door and recognised him.

'An honour to see you again, Corporal Crutch. A real honour. I'm afraid I have orders not to let you in or to let Abagail out.'

'I understand,' said Crutch. 'Can I just see the admiral?'

'The admiral's given me very specific instructions. That's not possible.'

Crutch pushed past the corporal and banged on the door with his fist. 'Admiral Hastings, this is Corporal Crutch. Could you please come out here and talk to me?'

The guard unsheathed his sword. Crutch looked him in the eye and said, 'I stood in the burning rigging of an Estovian ship in the siege of Ironbay and fought off the whole crew trying to kill me. I stood against three thousand Estovian soldiers on the Kona track, cut the head off their general, and sent it back to Estovia in a sack. Do you really wanna fight me?'

The guard backed away. 'No. No, I don't.'

Crutch turned back to the door. 'Admiral Hastings!'

The admiral opened the door. Abagail and Lady Hastings were behind him. Abagail tried to run out the door, and the admiral caught her by the wrist to stop her.

'What is this?' said Admiral Hastings.

'I tried to stop him,' said the guard.

'It's not your guard's fault,' said Crutch. 'I apologise for being so loud, but I won't apologise for being here. There's something I have to say to you.'

'I'm listening,' said the admiral.

'I don't want to fight with you. After Zanithburg, and Papageenar, and Teevilgrad, I've done enough fighting. I know Abagail is your daughter. I know you want what's best for her. She's so special.

'Abagail stood on the docks in the rain when I left for the Kona Track, and she was there waiting for me when I got back. She sat with me at the Rosewood Cemetery day after day and never complained when it was only my body that was with her, not my spirit.

'Then Abagail found a way to help me live again. She gave me back my life, my hope.

'I spent weeks in Teevilgrad pretending to be someone I'm not. I've spent most of my life pretending. I can't pretend any more.

'I'm a commoner, a cripple. I'll never be a noble. I'll never know which fork or which spoon to use at the table. I don't even know what it's like to live in a house. But I love your daughter with everything I have, and I'll love her until the day I die.

Crutch fell to his knees, his voice fading to a last hopeless prayer, tears sliding down his cheeks. 'I survived the prison in Zanithburg. I survived the Kona Track. I survived Teevilgrad. But I can't survive without Abagail. Please, I'm begging you. Don't take her from me.' His head dropped. 'Don't take her from me.'

When he looked up, Abagail was there, kneeling in front of him. Abagail with that wonderful, crooked face now wet with tears. She put her arms around him.

'I'm here, Crutch. I'm here.'

Chapter 55
Love Is Love

The marines stood outside the door of office 451. Sergeant Zander looked over at Longshot.

'Is my hair good?'

'Yes, Sarge.'

'What about my uniform? How does it look? Is everything buttoned up right? Are there any creases?'

'You look great, Sarge. Best I've ever seen you.'

'You look like an admiral,' said Boulder.

Sergeant Zander did look great. He'd pressed and primped all morning to get ready for this meeting. It was barely noticeable, but Crutch could tell Sergeant Zander's hands were trembling.

'Here goes.' Sergeant Zander knocked on the door. Crutch could hear bolts pulled, locks unlocked, then the door opened and there was Jasper.

The portly male Jasper with the paunch at his belly and the moustache.

'Come in,' said Jasper in his very middle-aged, very male voice.

It was like Sergeant Zander was a water skin filled tight that someone just stuck a knife in. His face and his shoulders dropped.

Jasper turned and relocked the door. Sergeant Zander stood watching, his face a picture of disappointment.

'Now,' said Jasper. 'This is a special occasion. You are all to receive exceptional service medals, the highest award of the Secret Office.'

'There's a Secret Office?' said Crutch.

'No,' said Jasper, smiling.

'As I said, you've all been awarded the exceptional service medal of the Secret Office.'

'Which doesn't exist,' said Quicksilver.

'You're getting better at this Quicksilver.'

'I like medals,' said Boulder. 'They give you cake.'

'Indeed, they do Boulder. And just for you, we have your favourite cake.'

Boulder grinned when he saw the cake on the desk behind Jasper.

'Now if you could all line up for the presentation.'

'We're doing it here?' said Longshot.

'Oh no. I don't know how it slipped my mind. We're going down to the town square. There'll be a marching band, and the whole population of Ironbay will turn out to cheer on the secret heroes of Teevilgrad who don't exist for a covert operation that never happened.'

'When you put it like that,' said Longshot.

Jasper laughed. 'Sorry Longshot. You all deserve the parade. You really do. You pulled off what might be the most successful mission in the history of the Secret Office. I don't know that, of course, because…'

'The Secret Office doesn't exist,' said Quicksilver.

'You've finally got the hang of this Quicksilver. Now if you could all please stand at attention.'

'Attention,' said Sergeant Zander, and the marines pulled into a straight line, bodies taut and chests out.

Jasper went along the line, pinning a round gold medal to each of their chests. Quicksilver was first.

'For exceptional service. Congratulations and well done.'

'Thank you, Jasper.'

Jasper pinned the medal on Boulder's chest.

'For exceptional service. Congratulations and well done.'

'Do I get cake now?'

'Soon Boulder.'

Jasper came to Quicksilver.

'For exceptional incendiary service,' said Jasper.

'Does that mean fire?'

'Yes,' said Jasper.

Quicksilver smiled. 'Thank you very much.'

Then Crutch.

'There's always a place for you here in the Secret Office,' said Jasper.

'Thank you, Jasper,' I'll stick with the marines. I want to spend a lot more time at home in Ironbay.

Jasper smiled. 'I know Abagail will appreciate that. Great work, Crutch. Your operation will go down in the history of espionage. The Secret Office won't be talking about it for years.'

'Because they don't exist,' said Crutch.

'You are my best student,' said Jasper. 'That other thing you asked about.'

'Yes?' said Crutch.

'Go to the Unity Hall at seven o'clock any night.'

'Thank you,' said Crutch, smiling.

Jasper pinned a medal on Longshot.

'For exceptional service. Congratulations and well done.'

'Thank you, Jasper. We couldn't have done it without you.'

'My brains, your bravery. You earned a dozen medals.'

Jasper came to Sergeant Zander, who looked at him awkwardly.

'For truly, truly, exceptional service Sergeant Zander. Congratulations and very, very well done.'

Crutch glanced over. He'd never seen Sergeant Zander blush before.

'A round of applause for the medal recipients,' said Jasper. They stood there in silence. 'You have to clap now.' The marines applauded themselves, and Jasper joined in smiling proudly.

'Now you've basked in the glory of appreciation from the Secret Office, I have to take those medals back.'

'Take them back?' said Longshot.

'The Secret Office doesn't exist. A Secret Office that doesn't exist can't be giving out medals.'

Jasper went along the line, unpinning the medals. 'You may get these back. Files in the Secret Office are sealed, usually for thirty years. When they're opened, medals and other valuables are returned to their owners.'

'So we get our medals back in thirty years?' said Longshot.

'If you're alive then, and if the files for this mission are unsealed.'

Jasper got to Sergeant Zander. As he unpinned the medal on Sergeant Zander's chest, he said, 'Would you like to join me later for a…debriefing?'

'Will you be…dressed differently?'

'Mmm hmm.'

Sergeant Zander smiled and blushed again as Jasper slipped a piece of paper into his trouser pocket.

'And now we can have cake,' said Jasper.

'I like cake,' said Boulder.

As they left the navy office building, Crutch said, 'So you're seeing Jasper tonight?'

'Yes,' said Sergeant Zander, clinging to the piece of paper in his trouser pocket and smiling.

'It's nice when two people love each other,' said Longshot.

'Very nice,' said Quicksilver.

'Even if they're… '

'Even if they're what?' said Sergeant Zander.

'You know,' said Longshot.

'Oh, for pity's sake,' said Sergeant Zander. 'Jasper is a woman.'

'We could see that today,' said Quicksilver.

'You don't have to be embarrassed about it,' said Longshot.

'Love is love,' said Boulder.

Crutch realised that he and Sergeant Zander were the only marines who'd seen Jasper as a woman. He also realised Jasper wanted it that way. For whatever reason, she didn't want the navy and government in Ironbay to know who she really was. She was a true master of espionage. Even her own government couldn't give away her true identity.

'Crutch, help me out here. Tell them Jasper is really a woman.'

'Sergeant Zander is telling the truth,' said Crutch, grinning. 'You saw Jasper today. She's obviously a woman.'

'Thanks a lot,' said Sergeant Zander.

'Any friend of yours is a friend of ours,' said Longshot.

'My mam always used to say, never shy away from who you really are,' said Quicksilver. 'Even if other people don't like it.'

'Love is love,' said Boulder.

Sergeant Zander gave up.

'When did your mam tell you not to shy away from who you really are?' said Longshot.

'When I was in jail for burning down the local guard house.'

'That explains a lot,' said Longshot.

Chapter 56
We Danced

It took a week of practicing every night, but tonight he was ready. Crutch took Abagail to the Unity Hall at seven o'clock. Tagging along with them was Corporal Levi, their chaperone. Something Abagail's father insisted on now, any time they went out at night.

'It's all very mysterious,' said Abagail.

'I told you it's a surprise,' said Crutch.

'I like surprises,' said Abagail.

'I think you'll love this one.'

When they entered the large hall, Novaleev walked over the wooden floor to him.

'Crutch. I'm glad you made it,' said Novaleev. 'And this must be Abagail. She's even more beautiful than you told me.'

'Thank you,' said Abagail, smiling uncertainly.

'And who is this?' said Novaleev, looking at Corporal Levi.

'This is our chaperone, Corporal Levi,' said Crutch.

'You won't be needing that sword tonight, Corporal Levi,' said Novaleev.

'I'm required to wear it,' said Levi.

Novaleev raised his eyebrows and turned back to Abagail.

'Did Crutch tell you what we do here?' said Novaleev.

'No. He said it was a surprise.'

'What a wonderful surprise,' said Novaleev. 'I won't keep you in suspense any longer then. What do we do, people?'

The group of people milling around in the hall behind him yelled in unison, 'We dance!'

'We dance,' said Novaleev.

'Really?' said Abagail.

'Yes, of course. Dancing is a gift to your body, your mind, and your soul.'

'But Crutch…'

'Crutch is a wonderful dancer,' said Novaleev. 'As you will see.'

'I knew you loved dancing, so I've been practicing,' said Crutch.

'Really?' said Abagail.

'Really,' said Crutch.

'But how?'

'You'll see,' said Crutch.

'Form a circle!' said Novaleev. 'Come join us, Corporal Levi.'

Crutch joined the circle of dancers, with Novaleev on one side and Abagail on the other. Corporal Levi joined the circle with some trepidation, but when two attractive young women joined arms with him, he smiled.

An old man with a stringed instrument started playing, slow and steady at first.

Half the people in the hall stood and clapped in time with the rhythm.

Novaleev called out, 'Left, left, left.'

The people clapping yelled, 'Hey!' and Novaleev called out, 'Right, right, right.'

Two rounds through that, and they didn't need any more direction. Crutch looked into Abagail's eyes and smiled. She smiled and laughed right back as she danced.

The music sped up, faster and faster. Crutch kept looking right into Abagail's eyes. She struggled to keep up as the circle went faster, but she loved the struggle.

Finally, the music stopped, and everyone burst into applause.

'We danced,' said Abagail her eyes filled with joy.

'We danced,' said Crutch and took Abagail into his arms.

Thank You
Please Read

As an author, I want to thank you from the bottom of my heart for reading my novel. Without you, the reader, there would be no novel. You make it possible for me to practice the craft I love.

If you enjoyed this novel please consider rating and reviewing it on Amazon. Leaving a review on Amazon is the single most powerful thing you can do for an author with their novels listed there. It helps the novels become more visible on the site which leads to more sales and downloads.

My genuine thanks again for reading this novel.
Andrew Cavanagh

Novels by Andrew Cavanagh available on Amazon include:
Ironborn: Book #1 in The Ironborn Saga
Our Blood Our Land: Book #2 in The Ironborn Saga
Igor's Kitchen: Book #3 in The Ironborn Saga
True Royals: Book #4 in The Ironborn Saga
With more to come.

Download Your FREE Novella:
Wyld Vengance: Prequel to The Ironborn Saga
is available FREE at andrewcavanagh.com

Printed in Dunstable, United Kingdom

65663993R00127